# AETHERBOUND

# AETHERBOUND

BY E. K. JOHNSTON

DUTTON BOOKS

**DUTTON BOOKS**

An imprint of Penguin Random House LLC, New York

First published in the United States of America by Dutton Books,
an imprint of Penguin Random House LLC, 2021

Visit us online at penguinrandomhouse.com.

Library of Congress Cataloging-in-Publication Data is available.

Book manufactured in Canada

ISBN 9780735231856

1   3   5   7   9   10   8   6   4   2

Design by Anna Booth

Text set in Adobe Caslon Pro

*To Josh, who has believed this was a book since it was a text message of four bees.*

**CONTENT WARNING:**

*This book contains a scene of medical violence.*
*Characters also obsess about food and count calories.*

*Take your broken heart.*
*Make it into art.*

—CARRIE FISHER

# AETHERBOUND

W hen the Stavenger Empire turned its eyes to the stars, seeking new worlds to conquer, it found exactly what it was looking for. Planet after planet came under the imperial banner, the conflict providing impetus for the original warring Stavenger states to stick together as the empire grew. Worlds that could support life were colonized. Worlds that could not were stripped of their resources and left spinning in the dark. And then the armada reached the edge of the Stavenger solar system, looked at its great æther-workers, and wondered what it was going to do next.

The star-mages had the answer. There were so, so many stars, after all, and some were closer than others, and therefore reachable. The metal-mages used the æther to build ships and the grain-mages used the æther to stock them, but the travelers themselves were wary: The distance was so vast, and the destinations largely unknown. The Stavengers cried out for a hero, and they got one. A new kind of mage, one who could combine metal and sky, making Wells to hurl ships over the vast distances and Nets to catch them when they arrived. It was dangerous and it took all the years of the mage's life—not to mention several generations of her descendants'—but when the Well-and-Net relay was done, there were seven bright stations between the Stavenger system and that of their target, the Maritech. A journey that might have taken generations at normal sublight speeds now took days of quick jumps that crossed distances so vast, the mind could scarcely comprehend them.

The first Stavenger ships that landed in the Maritech Net were not ungreeted. It's hard to conceal such a large construction project, after all, even if you are using magic. The Maritech knew that they were coming, and met them in force. Five times the great waves of the Stavenger armada broke into Maritech space, and five times they were repelled. Not even æther gave the Stavengers an edge, for the Maritech had a form of it themselves. A few foolhardy mining ships were able to sneak through the lines and collect gasses from the outer planets in the system, but no Stavenger ship so much as pierced atmosphere on an inhabited Maritech world. The empire, humiliated, withdrew, and the Maritech destroyed the station that supported the last Net in the relay, so that no jump could ever be caught (the only logical conclusion after none of the adventurous ships that made the jump from Brannick Station ever returned).

Determined to salvage something from their disastrous effort to colonize the stars, the failing Stavengers began exploiting those resources that could be found near the remaining space stations they had built. Initially restricted to asteroid mines and the odd nebula for gas collection, Stavenger ships soon began encountering huge numbers of a space-going creature they called *oglasa*. At first the creatures were just slaughtered to clear the space lanes (which will give astute observers an idea of *how many* there were), but eventually some scientist analyzed the remains and realized that the Stavengers had, almost entirely by accident, discovered the most perfect food source in the known universe.

The oglasa were massacred. Billions of tonnes of them were caught in the blackness of space and brought to the stations for processing. The stations, meant to be merely way stations and restocking points for traveling armies, were redesigned to house trade at the levels in the capital of the Stavenger homeworld. Oglasa were almost pure protein—which the æther-workers needed to perform their magic—and contained enough vitamins A, C, and D to prevent the two most common immunodeficiencies found on long-haul space travel. And it didn't go bad. Ever.

The Stavengers no longer needed Wells and Nets to travel through the farthest distances of space. Instead of building expensive installations, ships could now be stocked with enough food to last the journey. Instead of spending the lifetimes of dozens of mages building one road, they could spend the lifetimes of thousands of colonists creating hundreds.

A properly supplied and coordinated colony ship could be sent out at regular sublight speeds, and the crew could just reproduce until they got where they were going, as long as the ship stayed sound and those aboard it kept track of their stores.

Plans were made. Designs were drawn. Calories were counted. Colonists were screened for suitability. And then disaster struck.

A burst of unknown radiation erupted out of the Stavenger sun, and swept through space at an almost scientifically impossible rate. It left organic matter unharmed and electronics unburned. It didn't interrupt sound waves or fritz out the invisible pathways by which information was transmitted.

But the æther was fried. Even the greatest living masters of magic struggled to muster enough power to boil an egg, and since there were easier ways to heat water, they didn't try. Only magic that had already been done remained.

Fortunately, this included the Wells and the Nets, though they now had to be manually controlled from aboard each station. The seven stations saw their chance and took it, desperately trying to secede from the empire as the armada was drawn back to the homeworld to protect the aristocracy from insurrection. Despite the stations' bravery and general good timing, the empire had one last blow to strike. The most powerful remaining Stavenger grain-mages were stuffed to the gills with all the food they could stomach, and then forced to spend their life's energy on one last great work.

So the stations' rebellion died—or at least died down. The economy shifted once the general die-off was over, and eventually some sense of order returned. The Empire fell apart, but their successors formed a complicated hegemony to exert power over the home system, and continued to bicker amongst themselves over who should benefit most from the wealth collected from the stars. Parts of the armada had been abandoned in space when magic was broken, and to survive, the crews of those ships turned to depravities best left unmentioned.

On the stations, life continued. The oglasa were a memory, too far away to reach, and so the people scratched out resources from asteroids and gas clouds and hoped against hope that the mines would last forever.

And gradually, gradually, gradually, the æther healed, and the magic came back.

# PART ONE

"YOU'LL NEVER LEAVE
HARLAN ALIVE"

# 1.

**THE FIRST TIME PENDT** Harland saw the stars, she was five years old. She was watching her brothers play Spark in the crèche on board the *Harland*, where the Family children learned ship operations in the guise of competitive play, and the lines of alliance formed before teeth were cut. Pendt couldn't play Spark. Or, she could, but she lost every time and so no one wanted to be on her team. She couldn't make the cards light up yet, activating the necessary circuits to identify a match in her opponent's hand, let alone find the set in her partner's. She was a liability, and so she always sat out. On the bright—ha!—side, this gave her more time to study the less popular aspects of the *Harland*. While her brothers learned to run the engines, Pendt taught herself everything she could about interstellar travel itself.

It was a strange thing, knowing oneself useless at five. Space was dark and cold, and worked against life in most of its forms. For a human to be in space while also being a liability was dangerous, for the human and for everyone around her. Pendt did her best to stay out of the way, and to excel wherever she could. Her bed was always made the most neatly. She always scraped her plate the cleanest, getting every trace of protein from the meal. She cleaned up the crèche if her brothers or cousins forgot something, and she always volunteered to run errands when a messenger was called to run belowdecks. Pendt avoided the captain, but there was no avoiding the first mate: She was Pendt's mother, and they shared quarters.

The day that Pendt saw the stars was the same as every other day since the *Harland* had set out into deep space. Pendt had been born shortly after their departure and knew no world but the grey metal that lined the innermost hull.

Sometimes her mother was kind and warm—cuddling under blankets in those last few moments before the alarm went off and made them rise for the day—but more often she was the *Harland*'s first mate, and had no higher loyalty than to its captain. Her children must grow quickly, as their cousins had, and earn a place on the ship. Her oldest boy, Kaeven, was ten years old, and they went down like rungs on a ladder to Pendt.

All of the children tensed the moment Lodia Harland entered the crèche. As a matter of survival, all Harland children could tell when their mothers were being Family or Officer. The captain was rarely Family, but Lodia was softer, and with her there was always a dreadful moment of uncertainty. Today, as Pendt examined her mother's face, she found no answers there. Lodia was a strange mix of Officer and Family both.

"Pendt," Lodia said. "Come with me."

Pendt was moving by the time her mother finished saying her

name. Behind her, Willam found a match in Antarren's hand, and Rheegar immediately began to accuse the twins of cheating.

"If we can do it, and if it doesn't cost, it's allowed," said Willam, and Rheegar conceded the match with an angry glower while the twins crowed and little Tyro looked grateful he was also sitting out and wasn't forced to pick a side. Kaeven was too dignified for squabbling and stayed out of it.

For her part, Pendt felt nothing, no glimmer of the pull that circuits and spare parts always mustered in her siblings. Her youngest cousin, Karderee, sat by the door reading an engineering manual. He was eleven, and was too old for Spark now. Soon Kaeven would join him, and then they would both disappear to the engine room forever. Now Karderee settled for sniffing disdainfully at Pendt as she went to answer her mother.

"Good luck, little cat," he said, a sneer twisting his mouth.

In the early days of space travel, there had been a cat on board every ship to hunt vermin. Now there were environmental filters for that, and cats were an outdated luxury, another mouth to feed. Pendt was never sure if her family meant the name as an insult, though it did seem like her cousins felt that way.

Pendt raised her chin and took it like a Harland. Lodia squeezed her hand, just a little bit, and pulled her out of the crèche.

The *Harland* was a transport ship, specializing in living cargo. Primarily, they took workers and supplies out to the mines and brought back raw ore for processing. The ship was old, too old for the engines to propel it quickly. A new vessel might make the same run in half a decade, while the *Harland* was set to spend eighteen years in space. But what the *Harland* lacked in speed, it made up for with size. The new ships were fast and small, and so they couldn't carry the sheer bulk of materials and people that the outer reaches required. That was how the Harlands had made their name: each generation born into the cycle of travel with a captain to lead them and engineers to keep the power flowing. They never stayed still long enough to spend much currency, it was said, but they were worth a lot of it.

Despite the size of the ship, Pendt spent most of her time in either her mother's small suite, the mess, or the crèche. The medical bay was visited only in emergencies, and Pendt had rarely been ill in her few years. When she took messages below, she went only as far as the hard-seal door that prevented any of the paying passengers from gaining access to the ship. Conditions belowdecks could be very rough, especially as the years wore on and the food and water down there ran low. It wasn't a very safe way to travel, and it was only moderately safer for the working crew, so the door was sealed against any and all incursions. The only exit they had below was to space, and the only news they ever heard was messages from the ship's microphone. Pendt took the job seriously, mouthing the words written on the datapad she was given without really understanding them. The text was all times to destinations, perhaps meant as a morale boost and an indication that the bleakness would not last forever. When she spoke her words into the microphone, they were relayed or they were not. She had no way of knowing.

In truth, she knew very little about the ship or their mission, save that both were vitally important, though to whom she had no idea. Much of the galaxy was beyond her, which was only fair given that no one ever told her anything worth knowing, except sometimes by accident. She knew that the bare minimum of supplies had been brought along, and must be carefully dealt with. There were opportunities for trade every few years when the *Harland* arrived at a mining colony, but preparation and rationing were of the utmost importance.

"A generation ship is only as good as the next generation," the captain would say, both as praise and condemnation. This was the only reason Pendt could see why her mother had six children to the captain's four. Ten mouths to feed was a serious investment, and the captain expected them to pay off even if she was too busy to give birth herself.

Today, as Lodia pulled her into the lift, Pendt felt fear for the first time in her life. Space was always fraught with some measure of uncertainty—either the void would get her or it wouldn't—but it didn't truly frighten her. And despite their best efforts, she was not afraid of her brothers or her cousins. But something about today was different, and on a spaceship, different was usually a bad thing. The lift moved in response to Lodia's bio-code, not Pendt's, which was much more restricted.

Pendt looked up at her mother, a hundred questions on her tongue, but she saw that Lodia had fully become the officer as the lift began to climb. Harlands didn't speak to officers unless they were spoken to. Instead, Pendt counted decks. They passed engineering, which Pendt had only seen in pictures. It covered several levels, both due to the size of the engines and the number of operations controlled there. Everything from air and water to light and the intercom was routed through the power sources there and

tended to by Pendt's oldest cousins and those born in Lodia's generation who hadn't reproduced.

Above Engineering was the deck where the non-Family crew
members lived. Pendt had only ever seen the ones who worked in
the galley. Anyone wishing to move to a colony could book passage
on a ship like the *Harland* or try to get hired. The crew had better
quarters and rations than those who just handed over currency
and tucked in to enjoy the ride. Those passengers were kept below:
out of sight, out of mind. The crew didn't necessarily know much
about ships, so the jobs they did were the least desirable ones on
board: cooking, cleaning, basic maintenance. The only exception
was Dr. Morunt, a haggard-looking woman who had been added
to the roster during a rare trip to Katla Station long before Pendt
was born. Pendt never knew quite what to make of the doctor. She
had a way of looking at her that made Pendt uncomfortable.

Last came three massive levels of stowage, where the captain
kept the items she was delivering, the supplies she rationed, and,
eventually, the ore she—or her descendant—hauled in from the
stars. It was sealed almost as tightly as belowdecks, and no one was
permitted in without clearance. Pendt had never been tempted.

The lift slowed, and then stopped at the bridge level. Pendt felt
a swirl of emotions: dread, excitement. She had never been there,
but she didn't know *why* she had been summoned. Not knowing was a weakness, and no weakness could be tolerated in space.
Lodia released her hand and straightened to attention. Pendt cop-
ied her without thinking about it. Harlands stood up straight. As
much as she could, and in all the ways that she could understand,
Pendt tried to be the perfect Harland.

"Be good, little cat," Lodia whispered as the door hissed open.

Her mother's voice was half admonishment, half desperate prayer. Pendt never misbehaved and didn't understand why her mother might think she would start now, of all times. Pendt stood up even straighter, and willed herself to look as calm and old and capable as a five-year-old can look. Her back straight, Pendt Harland took her first steps towards the true centre of her small grey world.

Pictures of the *Harland*'s bridge didn't do it justice. The workstations gleamed silver under the lights, and the toggles and buttons and screens seemed to promise adventure. Pendt, used to only as much light as was required, blinked against the brightness of it. Important work must be done here, if the captain needed so much light to do it. Here courses were plotted and schedules were made, long-range communiqués were answered and sent, and all the most important decisions were made.

And the noises! There was the hushed murmur as two officers—some of her mother's other remaining cousins—did their work. The steady tone of the navigation system, beaming light back out to the stars. The hum, even now, of the engines.

And at the centre of it all, the tall, uncompromising figure of Captain Arkady, standing at her terminal and issuing commands.

"Pendt," said the captain.

Out of the corner of her eye, in the fraction of a second before she turned to face her aunt, Pendt saw a screen—no, it wasn't clear enough for a screen: It was an actual porthole. It was clear steel, as strong as the rest of the hull but transparent and *much* more expensive.

And through it, she saw a thousand specks of light.

# 2.

"IT'S BEAUTIFUL, ISN'T IT?" Arkady said, her own gaze slipping from Pendt's face to the stars.

"Yes, sir," Pendt replied.

The window was why her aunt commanded the *Harland*. She could tell, with precision and certainty, where the ship was in relation to the stars at each moment. Lodia could do the same thing, but her sense of direction wasn't as good, so she was only the XO. She could hold a course, but she couldn't set one. Pendt dragged her eyes away from the stars to her aunt's face with some effort, and Arkady nodded.

"You know," she said, "I can't play Spark either. Neither can your mother."

"I know, sir," Pendt said. "You two can feel where we are, like the Stavenger sky-mages before magic was purged. That's why you're the captain and why Mother is allowed to have so many children."

None of Pendt's cousins had star-sense, and so far, none of Lodia's children did either. For the first time, Pendt wondered whether her mother might have another baby, even if it went off plan. A ship full of engineers needed a captain, and without a captain, the *Harland* would be lost in the void.

"That's right," said Arkady. Her voice was calm and level, not commanding. She was almost, almost, an aunt, except that her shoulders were held too high for her to be entirely family. "Some give their hands to the *Harland*, and some give their minds. Can you give something for our ship?"

"Of course, sir," Pendt said. Her chest puffed out. None of her brothers had been asked to do something for the captain yet, and she was the youngest of them.

"Eat this," Arkady said, and passed her a four-gram protein cube.

Extra food was unheard of on the *Harland*. If Pendt was eating it, that meant someone else was *not*, and there were only so many calories given to a person every day. As captain, and because her work took so much out of her, Arkady received the largest share. She must always have calories to burn, because she must always use the æther to know where they were and where they were going. Pendt received enough to make sure that she grew, and nothing more. She wanted to eat the protein slowly, to savour the treat, but something in the atmosphere of the bridge told her that this was not the time to dawdle. The older cousins were disciplined, of course, but she could still feel them watching her.

Pendt put the cube on her tongue and then ground it between

her teeth as quickly as she could. She swallowed, and for the first time in her short life, felt the whisper of potential in her mind.

"Pendt"—Arkady's voice had changed. Now she was the captain entirely, and this was a command, not a request—"I need you to make your eyes blue."

All of her siblings had blue eyes, and most of her cousins did too, except for Tanith, whose eyes were brown. Pendt's eyes were green. She usually did her best not to think about them. She only saw her reflection briefly every day when she brushed her teeth. On a ship where everyone important had the same utilitarian haircut and variations on the same genetics, green eyes were enough to mark her as an outsider within her own family, and she had never liked that feeling. Still, she couldn't imagine why the *Harland* needed her to have blue eyes. She knew she owed the ship already, even if she was only small. If she could help, she would.

It was like Spark, a bit, only instead of looking at circuits for a match, she was looking at a code, and the code was inside of her. She had never understood the game the way her brothers explained it to her, but this made much more sense than their muddled attempts to include her in their play. She saw the paths of light, the same as they described them. There was even a touch of electricity to it, but there was something else too, something that Pendt knew in her heart even if she couldn't put a word on her lips.

She found the part of the code that made her eyes green, and focused on it. She knew what blue looked like, both in someone's eye and in the code, even though no one had ever explained it to her, because her blue-eyed cousin was standing close by. She reached for that blue, strengthened by the four grams of protein, and wrote it overtop of her own green code. It felt as natural as breathing to do it, but experiencing the change made her uncomfortable in a way she couldn't articulate. How could something so easy feel so wrong? Was she going to be the same person after this? What right had she to do it, and what right had her captain—her aunt—to ask.

She opened her eyes, and Lodia gasped, a soft sound that might have been a sob, except Harlands didn't cry. The captain's face hardened.

"Pendt, you must listen to me," she said. Her tone was unmistakable now. Arkady had stopped thinking of her as Family and saw her only as part of the *Harland*.

"Yes, sir," Pendt said.

She didn't know what she had done wrong. She had done exactly as Arkady asked. Maybe it was the wrong shade of blue. She couldn't see her own eyes, of course, but Pendt was sure she'd matched her cousin's eye colour when she'd changed the code. Maybe she should have gone with Arkady's shade instead. Maybe her aunt had wanted her to be more creative. Pendt tried reaching for the blue again, and she could see it just as clearly as before, but something inside her *knew* that if she tried again, without the protein, it would only hurt her in the long run.

"You must never use your gene-sense again," Arkady said, giving name to Pendt's curse. "Do you hear me? Never use the æther, unless I have given you permission."

"You mean until I get lessons?" Pendt asked. Surely there was a version of Spark for her to play, now that she knew what she could do. The colours called to her, choice beyond measure, and she couldn't answer that call. "I've been doing my best to instruct myself until—"

"I mean never," said the captain, abruptly cutting her off. It wasn't the colour. It was the fact that she could do it. "Your skills will not be useful to the *Harland* until you come of age. Until then, you will do what you are told."

Pendt wanted to cry, but some instinct told her that crying wouldn't help, and she clung to it, even as her Harland-ness seemed to fall away from her. If she was useless, then there was *nothing* that would help. She would be a blue-eyed burden forever.

"I'm sorry, sir," Pendt said. Her voice was very small. "I'm sorry I'm not better. For the *Harland*."

"I am sorry too," Arkady said. She spoke like she'd already forgotten who Pendt was and didn't look in her direction. She looked at Lodia instead. "You're dismissed."

Pendt remembered nothing about the lift ride back down to Family quarters. Her mind was struggling to absorb everything she had seen: the lights and sounds, the coldness of her aunt's look, the way her cousins gazed right through her. Lodia didn't hold her hand.

"You only have bio-sense, nothing electrical or star-born, or even mathematical," Lodia said when she and Pendt got back to the Family quarters. "That's what gene-sense means. Before the æther was purged, the Stavengers called it grain-sense, and mostly used it for farming. We have no need of that here. It's not worth it to spend the calories on you."

Pendt said nothing. The part of her that wondered about

the future and dreamed about flying a ship with her siblings was dying, and the part that was growing in its place was a silent, waiting thing.

"You won't be useful until you're eighteen and can work legally under the shipborn rules," Lodia continued. "Then you can be hired out. Until then, you will be worthless. The captain will decide what you can do to earn oxygen."

Pendt understood only that she was useless, and that she didn't deserve to breathe as a result. She knew that eighteen was far away, more than ten years, and she knew exactly how many calories and how much atmosphere a person consumed in that much time.

Then her brain fixed on the word *hire*. They would get her a job on another ship. She'd have to leave everything and everyone she had ever known and go to a place where she wasn't Family. She would never belong again, and that was the worst fate she could possibly imagine. She wasn't much of a Harland, to her shame, but in all of her dire imaginings, she had never considered losing her name. She'd rather face the airlock.

The next morning, Pendt was taken to the galley instead of the crèche. She would miss the quiet times she'd spent learning about *Harland* operations, but she wouldn't miss her brothers. Or the way everything in the room reminded her that she was useless. Or the constant feeling of disapproval from whatever elder cousin was in charge of training. Really, she could read anywhere.

She was too young to be of good service doing maintenance, and the galley was moderately safer anyway, though Pendt was never sure if that had entered into Arkady's calculations. The children didn't get jobs until they were twelve unless they showed remarkable aptitude, and Pendt had no aptitude for anything. It was known immediately by everyone who saw her, family and otherwise, that her position was a mark of some terrible failure on her part.

The cooks made her stand on a stool to pass them things or carry pots that were too big for her. When she made mistakes, she was reported immediately for punishment. She didn't hold it against them. They would be punished far worse if they coddled her, and they had no reason to. Even shamed, Pendt was Family and they were not. That meant she was the Family's to use as they saw fit. Arkady ruled in the galley as much as she ruled everywhere else, and her edict regarding Pendt was wordless, but clear nonetheless. Still, she was small, and she was clumsy, so Pendt made many mistakes.

"There is nothing in the void," said Lodia as she locked Pendt into one of the supply closets for having dropped three grams of vege-matter on the galley floor on the fourth afternoon of her new life. It wasn't her last infraction. She didn't like the small space or the confining dark, but she was coming to appreciate the solitude. She'd been forced to eat the matter as part of her own rations, of course, so there hadn't been any waste, but such behaviour couldn't go unpunished. "You have to be more careful."

Pendt held her chin up and took it like a Harland.

Three days and two more stints in the cupboard after that, she overheard her cousins discussing if their mother was going to airlock her.

"It would be much more economical," Donalin argued. "Otherwise we're going to feed her all these years to bring us dinner. Usually, we make people pay us to do that, just for the privilege of being on our ship."

"She's still Family," Tanith said. She was sixteen, and there was something in her face that made Pendt think she knew a secret that would never even occur to her younger sister or any of the boys. "A Harland is always worth something, even if we have to wait for her for a bit."

"The captain has made it clear we're not to bother with her one way or the other," Jerrus said. He was the most practical of the lot, the most like his mother, except he couldn't feel the stars. "So, we won't, unless we get new orders."

"And you'd better set an example for her sibs," Tanith said. "Not to mention Karderee. They need to understand how fragile our balance is, and what Pendt's flaws might cost us."

That shut everyone up for a while. The Harlands were not afraid of space, but they were respectful towards it, and not a one of them, Pendt included, was going to tempt fate.

As she cleared plates from the table without being acknowledged by any of her relatives, it occurred to Pendt that she had one thing they didn't have: She had seen the stars.

She didn't see them again for a very long time.

# 3.

JUST BEFORE SHE TURNED eight, Pendt asked if she could work in hydroponics. She told her mother that she knew as much about plants as she did about protein—which was to say, not much—and that she thought she could help the plants grow better.

"How do you know that?" Lodia asked, and Pendt found herself the sole recipient of her mother's attention quite suddenly. It was not a reassuring feeling.

"I just"—Pendt groped for words to explain the feeling—"I just do?"

It was difficult to elucidate. It was similar to the feeling that Pendt had as she measured out calories onto her siblings' plates, but wilder and less predictable. She felt it most strongly when she had just eaten, and sometimes it knocked the wind out of her if she chased it for too long.

Lodia was quiet for a moment, and then she put her hands under Pendt's chin and forced her to make eye contact.

"You will always feel that call," Lodia said. Her voice was pure Officer, but there was a fear in her eyes that Pendt didn't understand. "I feel a call to the stars and your brothers feel the call of electricity, but you must *never* answer it, do you understand me?"

"But I can make the plants grow better," Pendt protested. "I know I can. I can be better for the *Harland*."

"The *Harland* has all the plants it needs," Lodia said. "The machines in hydroponics are sufficient to our needs, and they do not require calories like you would if you did their work."

Tears sprang to Pendt's eyes. She hadn't learned to control the impulse to cry yet, even though she was always determined to stop herself. She ground them off her cheeks with the palms of her hand and faced her mother.

"I want to be better for the *Harland*, sir," she said. "I'm sorry my idea is a bad one."

"It's all right, Pendt," Lodia said. "If you knew everything about ship operations at eight, it would be a miracle. It takes a long time to understand the balance of space. Your aunt works hard to maintain it, making sure we have exactly what we need and nothing more. That's how we survive."

Her mother opened the door to their quarters and ushered Pendt out into the hallway. It was past time for both of their shifts to start. Lodia was nearly due on the bridge to relieve the captain for the afternoon's inspection, and Pendt was, as always, to report to the galley.

"Will you leave me at the next colony?" Pendt asked just before her mother stepped into the lift. Her cousins had started whispering things about her being left behind. It was marginally better than when they suggested Arkady might just airlock her and get it over with.

"No, little cat," her mother said. The use of the name was not a comfort, less a bargain and more a threat. "When you're eighteen and can sign a contract on Brannick Station, you'll be worth so much to us."

That vague promise or something like it was all Pendt ever got. She didn't know why she would suddenly be worth more when she was eighteen, except that she would be able to enter into contracts. Her oldest cousins could do that if they wanted, though they didn't need one to work on the *Harland*. Dr. Morunt was under contract, but Pendt's mother never talked like she was planning to give her daughter medical training. The cook had no gene-sense to speak of, relying on Morunt's calculations to determine who ate how much. It must have something to do with food, though. Everything always came back to food.

Pendt continued to wonder about it while she worked in the galley preparing lunch. She was best at measuring out portions, so the job was usually given to her. This required much less heavy lifting, but she could still make mistakes by being imprecise or by dropping things, so her rate of punishment had not decreased.

Pendt fetched the containers from the galley stowage and arranged the trays being assembled for everyone's meal. Each tray had a coloured chip on it, indicating who the meal was for, and Pendt's job was to make sure the calories on the plate matched

Dr. Morunt's recommendations. The food was divided up by type: protein, vegetable, starch. Each package was made of fibres that would be recycled into wires and such. When it was emptied and cleaned, Pendt put it into the compressor. All told, it was tedious work. But it didn't result in getting burns from the stove and there was no point in complaining, so Pendt did it.

Sometimes, Pendt's life felt like an eternity of peeling back lids and scooping out the nutritious matter inside. The rational part of her knew that it had only been a few years and that she had too many more to get through to be thinking so defeatedly, but occasional irrationality was her only escape, and so when her job was particularly boring, she let herself drift while she was doing it.

The spatula scraped against the bottom of the container Pendt was holding, and she added it to her stack of empties. There were enough to put through the recycler—a machine that extracted the last bits of edible calories from the packaging and sent them to hydroponics for use as fertilizer—so Pendt added that to her rhythm. As they started to emerge from the recycler, Pendt placed the sanitized containers into the compressor, the last time she had to worry about them. Her attention split between the trays, the recycler, and the compressor, Pendt did not anticipate the danger she was in until it was too late.

She reached a fraction of a centimetre too far into the compressor or maybe she withdrew her hand a fraction of a second too late. She never knew. It didn't matter. What mattered was that her index finger got caught in the gears that controlled the speed of the machine.

Time seemed to slow down, and she was aware that what was about to happen was going to hurt. A lot.

Her finger was crushed between two pieces of metal and she screamed. She pulled her hand back, but the nail caught on a jagged edge, and tore all the way off. She turned away from the trays, determined to bleed only on the floor, and cradled her hand against her chest. Her jumpsuit turned red and the cook and the other galley workers were screaming at her, but she couldn't understand them. All she knew was pain.

It was in her hand, in her finger. It was dripping out of her onto the floor and soaking into her shirt. The pain was everywhere, but it was also laser-focused in her fingertip, and her fingertip was something she could reach.

Without meaning to and beyond all control, Pendt sank into the code she usually worked so hard to ignore. She found the part of her that hurt and saw the magic that would make the hurting stop. It was behind a wall. A barrier she wasn't strong enough to climb. Pendt thought about giving up, about letting the pain take her, but the temptation to fix herself was too much.

Pendt smashed through the wall. It took everything she had, and she dropped to her knees. Her hair withered against her scalp and her skin felt raw and dry. On the other side of the wall was her fingernail, whole and new. Pendt put it on her hand, wincing as the new growth cut over the forming scab.

Her blood rushed through her, and now it all stayed in her veins like it was supposed to. This was what it felt like do magic. This was how her aunt felt when she touched the stars. The cruelty of her denial stung even more now that Pendt felt what she was missing. It was euphoric. It was incandescent. It sparked through her like fire and whispered to her soul like smoke.

It was the last thing Pendt thought about before she collapsed on the floor of the galley, the pristine food trays ready for lunch and the carnage of her accident spread out around her.

"—has to control it!" Arkady was raging. Pendt stayed very still, her eyes firmly shut. "We can't have her growing fingernails every time she hurts herself. She's wasting too much energy."

Without seeing, it was hard to tell where she was. Everywhere on the *Harland* smelled the same, thanks to the air recyclers. There was a quiet beeping sound, just loud enough for Pendt to hear. That meant she was in medical.

"She can't help it, Captain," Morunt said. Definitely medical. The doctor rarely went into the mess, much less ate there. "Instinct took over the moment her pain centres overwhelmed her logic. She's too young to let herself hurt when she knows how to stop it."

"Then stop her," Arkady said sharply. "Your caloric allowance only goes so far, Doctor. You might as well help her to avoid extending yourself."

Pendt drifted out again, and when she woke up, she was alone. There was an IV in her arm, dripping calories into her body at a truly astounding rate as she recovered from the stress of what she'd done. Her hand was fine; the nail looked exactly like it had before she'd injured it. Her head was cold, and when she touched it with her free hand, she found that she was bald.

"You took all the energy you had," Dr. Morunt said from nearby. "It killed the roots of your hair. They weren't exactly gentle bringing you down here, and most of it fell out by the time you arrived."

"Thank you, Doctor," Pendt said. Her head felt like it was stuffed with insulation and her whole body ached, but she knew that was she alive because Morunt had done her job. Then, because this was all the sympathy she was likely to get, she added: "I don't understand what I did."

"You used your gene-sense to regrow your fingernail when you tore it off," Dr. Morunt told her. "You must be very careful to avoid injury. You're too young to react sensibly to it, and I'm not sure I'll be able to bring you back again."

Morunt looked pale, and Pendt understood from what she'd heard Arkady say that the calories pumping into her body had come out of the doctor's own rations. Pendt was glad she'd been unconscious for the part where her mother and aunt debated whether or not she was worth treating. There were things about her family she didn't ever need to know.

"I won't do it again," Pendt said. "I don't want to burden the *Harland* in any way."

There were more calories in her IV than Morunt could afford to give. They must have come from somewhere, and Pendt didn't want to know. She'd find out if her cousins cut it out of her skin later, she supposed, or when she was punished for what she'd done.

"I can show you, if you like?" Morunt said. "I can help you dull the instinct to use what you have."

Pendt was still young enough that all adults were considered old. For the first time, she realized how much older than her mother Dr. Morunt was. Surely a doctor would have a family somewhere, and yet here was Morunt, indentured on a generation merchant ship.

"You're stronger than I am, little cat," Morunt said. "In every way, I think. You'll be better at all of this than I was."

Morunt gave her needles that dulled the call of her power and taught her methods of pain management that didn't involve regenerating body parts. It was the first formal education in the use of her own power Pendt had ever received, even if it was based around not using æther at all. Neither of them ever mentioned it to the captain. Pendt soon grew proficient at inventing reasons to spend her sparse free time in the medical bay.

Arkady locked Pendt in the brig for a full week and removed her from her mother's quarters. Now Pendt lived in a small cubicle that had been a storage closet, and Tanith moved in with Lodia.

In the galley, Pendt no longer daydreamed. She had nothing to dream about, in any case. And she learned that she could hear what was being said in the mess if she stood in the right place and was quiet enough. That was how she found out the ultimate cost of her survival.

"Your argument was strong, Lodia," Arkady said. "I agreed to it in the heat of the moment, but I won't let you use Tanith or Donalin for this. None of their brothers can take over either of their jobs in the engine room. We can't run the ship without them right now, even if we limit the amount of time they spend off shift. It'll have to be you."

"It will be as you say," said Lodia.

Pendt didn't put all the pieces together until the ship came into Alterra, a mining colony in a gaseous nebula near an asteroid belt. She had wondered how the calories would be regained. She worried that the captain would change her mind and sell Pendt off ahead of schedule after all.

Instead, Captain Arkady traded the second-most valuable thing on the ship, and that is how Pendt got a baby brother.

# 4.

THE ALTERRA MINING COMPLEX had been on its last legs the last time the *Harland* had been there. That was almost two decades ago. There were countless rumours: The complex had dried up; a new asteroid had been located; pirates had taken over and used the mining tunnels as a base of operations. Arkady Harland ignored them all. It didn't matter who lived on Alterra these days, she pointed out. They'd need the supplies the *Harland* carried, and Arkady would buy anything that wasn't nailed down, if they let her. Especially food resources, to replace what Pendt had used up so recklessly just to save herself from pain.

Pendt was not privy to the captain's decisions, of course, but her cousins and siblings made sure to discuss it loudly when she brought them their meals. They weren't subtle enough to be vague about it, but they too lacked any real knowledge, so they speculated all manner of terrible fates for her as the ship closed in on its destination.

"We always dump passengers at Alterra," Rheegar said with all the authority of someone who had heard it from an adult. "Maybe they'll dump the galley cat too."

"Mother is going to keep her," Tanith said. She always sounded absolutely sure when she made this sort of declaration, though Pendt had not yet figured out why she was so certain. "We'll leave passengers, of course, or at least off-load some of the bodies, but the cat will stay."

There was grumbling at that. Her brothers and cousins usually mirrored the way the adults treated her. It had only been a few months since the fingernail incident, but most of them had switched from deliberate indifference to outright pretending she didn't exist. The younger family members were slower to change. They were too accustomed to having a reliable punching bag. They might have squabbled about Pendt's fate until the end of time, except that the *Harland* finally arrived at its destination, and they all found out.

Alterra was an asteroid. According to the stories passed around the complex, the mining colony was on its sixth or seventh asteroid out of the nearby belt. As each rock was exhausted of minerals or became unstable due to so much digging, it was shoved away, and a new asteroid was procured. Pendt did not really believe this. The asteroids were huge, and she'd never heard of that kind of magic. It would take a huge amount of fuel, and it would be very difficult to *stop* the asteroid once they got it moving.

Still, the complex was impressive. The Stavengers had built it, once upon a time—a giant spider of a construct, legs wrapped around stone—and the miners had done their best to keep it going.

Even Pendt could look that up in the *Harland*'s database. There were diagrams of how the port operated and maps detailing where merchants and their ships could dock. She did her best to picture the complex in her mind, but Arkady didn't encourage imaginative thinking, and so Pendt was mostly limited to memorizing the files in the brief moments of her day when she wasn't busy.

There was very little technical information in the files. Pendt didn't know what the complex was made of or how many people lived on it. She didn't know how the ore was extracted or where the miners were quartered. Only information pertinent to trading goods was provided, and even then, there was no indication of who, exactly, the captain would be trading with. Pendt didn't think to ask who owned the mine these days. In her mind, everything operated like the *Harland*, and people were born to wherever they were meant to work. And no one would have answered her anyway.

They came into one of the docking clamps slowly. It was the first time Pendt had ever done anything but move forward in space. She couldn't feel the minute changes in direction, not really, as Arkady brought the ship into port, but she could hear the engines rev and thrum with a new rhythm as the captain did her manoeuvres. Pendt wished she was important enough to be on the bridge, near her aunt's porthole. She wanted to see. At least her brothers were also stuck in the windowless engine room. They wouldn't be able to hold *that* over her.

The most unnerving moment was when the engines cut. Pendt fought off a wave of panic. In space, dead engines meant dead everyone. She'd imagined what quiet might feel like, but she wasn't ready for the absence of sound in her ears or the stillness of the deckplates under her feet. The airlock must have connected. The storage bay doors might even be open by now. Pendt could be breathing the first molecules of new-to-her oxygen in her life.

The clock in the galley chimed, pulling her thoughts away from such ridiculous fancies. It didn't matter where they were. Pendt's job hadn't changed, and it was almost time for dinner. Arkady would be gone, at least. The captain and her first officer would go to the complex for negotiations. Everyone else would go about their day almost as usual. There might be a bit less to do in the engine room, but there was never any possibility that Arkady would allow a single extra Harland off the ship.

Dr. Morunt appeared in the galley door. Pendt wasn't entirely sure how to behave. The doctor had started eating in the mess more frequently, but she mostly left Pendt alone, which made her the nicest person on board. Lodia had gone to see the doctor that morning, just before leaving the ship, and carried a thermo-sealed case with her when she left the medical bay. Pendt had seen her only briefly, but it was enough time for her to be curious about what her mother was up to. The case had made Pendt uncomfortable. She sensed two halves that could never be the same whole, similar to each other and yet different in key ways that she could not identify. Lodia had taken the case off the ship. Whatever was in it, Arkady must be willing to trade with Alterra.

"Your mother has new caloric requirements," Morunt said with no preamble. "Please ensure her portions reflect the changes."

She handed Pendt a datachip, which Pendt inserted into the galley computer. It was true. Lodia Harland's ration had been increased. There was no reason given, of course, but Pendt would not have asked questions anyway. She memorized the number automatically, instantly aware of how much food it represented. The computer readout told her that the difference would best be made up from the protein rations, not the vege-matter, but Pendt already knew that.

It wasn't the same as when she'd changed her eye colour or regrown the fingernail. That was a powerful surge, a sense of rightness and being that she couldn't deny. This was more of a comfort. A hug, if she'd ever received one. A reminder of what she could do, someday, and a reassurance that she hadn't lost the ability from not using it.

"Thank you, Doctor," Pendt said. "I will make the necessary adjustments."

Morunt looked at her with that close examination Pendt always found unnerving. It was like the doctor was waiting for her to figure something out, and Pendt wasn't thinking fast enough. If it was important, like Lodia's calories, Morunt would just tell her. Pendt was smart enough to realize that the doctor's reticence meant the information was, at least, a little illicit, and that it was up to her to put the pieces together. She couldn't expect Morunt to put herself out. So she did what she always did: She filed the information away, along with all her cousins' slights and her brothers' abuses, the hints she gleaned from the kitchen staff, and her own common sense, until she could figure it out.

"Do you want your meal now?" Pendt asked.

"Thank you." Morunt held out her hand. Pendt handed over the protein packet and the doctor's allotment of vege-matter, barely thinking as she measured it out. Morunt watched her as she scrupulously put the correct number of calories on the tray.

Pendt was about to ask a question, something inane like how long the doctor thought they would be at the station. She didn't get many opportunities for polite conversation, and Morunt was the only one likely to talk to her without speculating about her death. Before she could, the doors to the mess opened, and her brothers came in, looking for their meals as well.

Morunt retreated to the far corner of the mess, and Pendt turned her attention to making sure her brothers got the right food. Tyro was always hungry these days, wanting more than he was given. There hadn't been a change in his allotment, however, so Pendt quietly delighted in watching him covet what he couldn't have. She wasn't stupid enough to eat in front of him—no one would stop him if he tried to take some of her portion—but she did enjoy not being the *only* Harland who was miserable.

Tanith came in behind the boys, and Pendt gave her cousin her meal as well. They would never be friends, but as Pendt got older, Tanith seemed to pity her more, and that was better than scorn. Tanith looked at her plate, the portion measured out same as always, with an odd air of relief about her.

"Did Lodia get a calorie increase?" Tanith asked.

"Yes," Pendt said. Everyone would know the first time her mother came in for a plate, so there was no sense in hiding it.

"Good," Tanith said. "Better her than me."

That made no sense at all. She hadn't had a portion increase since she stopped growing. Anyone on the *Harland* would have welcomed more food.

Pendt considered it while she watched the others eat. The boys amused themselves by luridly speculating if the passengers down below had disembarked to work on Alterra or if they'd been off-loaded as corpses. The weight in the passenger compartment was down significantly, in either case. Pendt didn't like to think about it.

Finally, when her brothers and cousins were running out of excuses to hang around the mess, the doors opened and Arkady and Lodia came in. Everyone straightened; it was undoubtedly the captain who was about to address them. Lodia looked a little pale, and Pendt was immediately aware of something different about her, even though she didn't know what.

"You'll all be happy to know that I have secured a trade deal," Arkady said. "Not only have we replaced the food resources we lost"—here everyone glared at Pendt except the captain, who ignored her—"we have replenished our supplies enough to accommodate another Harland on board."

It took a moment for everyone to understand. Tanith looked blank. She was not surprised and was being very careful to keep her reaction to herself. The boys were immediately interested. Morunt kept her eyes on her plate, and the rest of the galley staff appeared similarly disinterested. The older cousins, the ones who were Lodia's age or older, looked at her with vague concern or interest, depending on who they were. And Pendt finally realized what they had stopped to trade at Alterra.

The food she had consumed to survive regrowing her fingernail had been recouped, purchased by the use of her mother's body for the growing of another Harland. That's why Lodia's calories had been increased, and that was the change Pendt could feel in her now. There was going to be another sibling. Another chance for a star-mage pilot. At the cost of Lodia's autonomy for nine months. And Tanith, old enough to carry children now, was relieved.

*Gene-mage.*

The words had haunted Pendt for the last few years, since the captain had declared her useless until she turned eighteen. For the first time, Pendt had a glimmer of understanding what her aunt's plan for her was. She looked at the doctor, meeting Morunt's gaze across the mess. Morunt's face was as carefully blank as Tanith's, but she gave Pendt a small nod. She was right. What was happening to Lodia right now loomed large in her own future. She looked at the trays in the galley, ready to go out into the mess for her mother and aunt.

Pendt had work to do.

# 5.

**TALBOR HARLAND WAS BORN** nine months later, just before Pendt's tenth birthday. He had ten fingers and ten toes, blue eyes, no hair to speak of, and he screamed all the time. Pendt was not terribly impressed with him. He felt the same as her brothers, though she couldn't have put words to what that meant.

"There's no real way to tell if a child is a star-mage or a gene-mage until they're old enough to talk to," Morunt explained while Pendt gave her her breakfast portion. It was almost as if the doctor was speaking to herself, but Pendt knew by now that it was the doctor's way of telling her to keep her thoughts to herself.

Pendt already knew that much. Captain Arkady had waited until Pendt was five years old to test her, after all, and she still had the blue eyes that marked her failure to reach the stars. She had known she wasn't an electro-mage by then, though: She couldn't play Spark.

All they could do was wait for Talbor to grow up and either

electrocute something unintentionally or learn to talk and reason, whichever came first. It gained her nothing to report her suspicions, so she didn't. Pendt was mostly unaware of the way time passed. She got older, and once in a while the computer informed her she was another year closer to being a legal adult. Now that there was a child to watch, though, Pendt became aware of all sorts of changes. Before, growth had been a nebulous thing, something that made her brothers more dangerous. With Talbor, it was much easier to mark the passage of time.

He held up his own head. He sat up without falling over. He crawled. He stood. He walked. Each change earned him an increased number of calories, and Arkady's continued surveillance. Eventually, he spoke. "More" and "Sir" and "Lodia," all in a garbled baby-soft voice that Pendt barely understood. She realized that she, too, must have had a first word, and that no one had cared to remember what it was.

When Talbor was two years old, he answered the question everyone had been not-asking since his birth. One day at lunch, he finished his allotted portion and screamed for more. None was to be given, of course, and so Pendt ignored his cries. He was old enough to sit and eat with his brothers now, strapped into a booster chair so he could reach the table and close enough to self-sufficiency that he was expected to practice. He was still a messy eater, by *Harland* standards, but he was already starting to learn that if he was careless, his belly went short.

When Pendt came to collect the empty trays, he stabbed her with his fork, blaming her for his hunger. He wasn't strong enough to hurt her, or at least he shouldn't have been. Pendt saw the whole thing in slow motion: the descent of the fork; the arc of pure electricity that jumped to her skin; her mother's private anguish; and her aunt's immediate disappointment.

"Ouch!" Pendt spoke reflexively, and immediately blinked to force the tears out of her eyes. Harlands didn't cry for this sort of thing.

"More!" demanded Talbor. He was capable of sentences, but rarely used them with Pendt.

"You'll get none," Arkady said.

Even at two, Talbor knew to shut up when the captain spoke. He threw his fork on the table but gave no further evidence of tantrum.

No one said anything else. If Arkady was angry, she didn't take it out on anyone. She looked at her sister and shook her head. Lodia stared at the table. Pendt's skin burned, but she stayed quiet too.

"Well, at least you'll be able to work in the engine room," Arkady said before the horrible silence dragged on too long. "Welcome to the *Harland*, Talbor."

Pendt had not been welcomed.

After that, the changes in Talbor were harder to keep track of, and Pendt stopped bothering to try. He was never going to love her, any more than anyone else in her family was going to love her, and she didn't really know how to try and make him love her anyway. His calories increased and she gave him his portion three times a day, and that was the extent of their relationship. He stayed in Lodia's quarters and Pendt stayed in her closet, and she wasn't miserable, at least.

After Talbor was seven or so, and Pendt was almost seventeen, two things happened on board the *Harland* that Pendt did keep track of. The first was personal: She started her menses. She had terrible cramps the first time, and thought was she was getting sick. She'd been afraid to tell anyone and had tried to do her job as normal, even though she was nearly doubled over by the pain. By now, she was a master of keeping her feelings to herself, but when the blood started, she finally had to go to the medical bay and see Morunt.

"Well, I suppose it was inevitable" was all Morunt said. "One more step."

Pendt hadn't expected any comfort but was relieved to know that her journey through puberty had been accounted for in the calorie allocations. For the first time in a while, her food ration was increased. It wasn't enough to allow her to do any magic, but it did grant her an awareness of her body that she soon came to appreciate. She couldn't make any changes to herself, let alone to anyone else, but she could see the pattern of her genes and *think* about possible changes, and that was the most practice she was likely to get.

Morunt gave her a painkiller and a shot of something that suppressed her bleeding until "it was time."

The second thing happened a few months later, when the *Harland* came into another colony. This one was definitely full of pirates, and Arkady kept the whole ship on lockdown as a result. She was willing to trade with them, of course, but they sure as hell weren't going to steal from her.

It was after lunch when Arkady returned from the port. The

boys had spent the meal with the usual chatter of whether the passengers below had disembarked or been dumped as so much dead weight. Usually, Tanith would shut them up, but she didn't this time, no matter how disgusting their speculation got. Lodia had come in only briefly for her portion, as had each of the adult cousins, before returning to the bridge. This port wasn't entirely safe, and all the grown-ups remained at their duty stations. Tanith should have to, Pendt thought, though it was possible that her mother had assigned her to keep her brothers from doing anything stupid.

When Captain Arkady walked into the mess, all conversation ceased immediately. The boys looked curious. Tanith looked at her plate. Pendt continued cleaning and sterilizing the food preparation surfaces in the galley but did her best to listen while she worked.

"Tanith, Pendt, with me," Arkady said.

Pendt nearly dropped the cleaning supplies. Instead she hastened to put them away. Arkady said nothing else to her daughter or her niece as she led them from the mess and down the corridor to the medical bay. Tanith moved woodenly, like her body was no longer hers to control. Pendt was too busy wondering why she was being brought along to give it much thought.

In the medical bay, Dr. Morunt stood by a cot that was prepped for one patient. A thermo-sealed canister sat next to the bed, along with a tray of medical tools.

"Strip," Arkady said to Tanith. It was definitely the captain speaking. There was no sign of anyone's mother.

For one horrible moment, Pendt thought her cousin would

refuse. No one *ever* refused Captain Arkady. But then Tanith jerked to movement, peeling away her jumpsuit and underclothes until she was naked.

"I don't know why you wanted Pendt," Arkady said to Morunt. Her tone was almost casual as Tanith got onto the cot and lay down, clearly beyond uncomfortable. Morunt injected her with something, and after a few moments, Pendt felt something shift in her cousin's body.

"I need her to confirm fertilization," Morunt said. "She's a bit more sensitive to that sort of thing than I am, I think, and since this is Tanith's first time, I wanted to be extra sure."

"Just get it done," Arkady said. "We've all got work to do."

Two tears leaked out of Tanith's eyes as Morunt made the insertion, but she made no noise at all. It must have been cold, at the very least, and Pendt couldn't imagine that it was comfortable, yet her cousin took it like a Harland.

"Well?" Arkady said.

"This method can take some time, Captain," Morunt said. "It's not like an implantation."

Pendt reached out, focusing her senses on Tanith's belly. The shifted thing she'd felt earlier was an egg, like the one she herself would release every cycle were she not taking suppressants. The injection must have unsuppressed Tanith. It was *time*.

Pendt felt other genes in her cousin's body, unfamiliar ones. That was what Morunt had inserted. Rather than a fertilized egg, like Lodia had received for Talbor, Tanith was simply being inseminated, and Pendt was there to confirm when it took.

"I don't have all day," Arkady said.

"Then you should have brought me a zygote," Morunt said. "But at this colony, we both know it's too dangerous for eggs to leave the ship, so you've done the next best thing, exposed the Family to less risk, and now we have to wait."

Arkady did not answer, but she didn't leave either. Instead, she stood and watched her daughter on the cot. Pendt wondered if maybe Tanith wanted someone to hold her hand but was not foolish enough to suggest it.

The minutes dragged by, and Pendt wasn't sure she would even know what it was she was supposed to sense. She could feel two halves, this time two halves that wanted to join with each other. She could tell the moment when they did, but even that wasn't the result Morunt was after. Arkady paced and Pendt was almost afraid to breathe. Still, Tanith made no noise and released no further tears. She didn't even shiver, and Pendt thought that she had to be cold by now. The medical bay was always a few degrees cooler than the rest of the ship, and Tanith was still naked.

And then it happened: implantation. Pendt knew it immediately, and inhaled sharply. Morunt put a hand on Tanith's belly and nodded. Pendt could see a vague shape of what the baby would look like but couldn't tell what, if anything, its æther connection would be. All she could feel was electro-sense, and that was what Tanith herself possessed. Arkady would not welcome that piece of news, and Pendt had no intention of being the one who told her.

"It's been successful," Morunt announced. "You can get dressed."

Arkady was looking at Pendt, and Pendt felt seen for the first time in years.

"You could tell immediately?" she asked.

"Yes, sir," Pendt said.

Arkady asked no more questions, and Pendt did not volunteer any additional information. Tanith dressed quickly, and Morunt updated her calorie allotment.

"You've done well, Tanith," Arkady said. There was no warmth in the captain's tone. It was a performance review and nothing more. "I am pleased."

"Thank you, sir," she said quietly. She looked like she wanted to vomit. "I'm glad I can serve the *Harland*."

"Teach Jerrus how to run the engine room," Arkady said. "You will be off for at least a week when the child is born, and someone will have to fill in for you."

With that, the captain left the medical bay. Tanith waited a few moments, and then went back to work too. She looked a little unsteady, but there was nothing wrong with her. Pendt waited until it was just her and Dr. Morunt.

"Did you know when I did?" she asked.

"No," said Morunt. "I didn't know until you gasped, and then I knew where to look. I always thought that you were stronger than I am, and now we know you are. I can only find things when I know where to look, and a lot of medical 'things' are very, very small."

"Can you fix them when you find them?" Pendt asked. She could clearly see the shifts in the pattern she'd have to make to change the baby to a star-mage. The scope of it frightened her too much to mention it, though.

"Not the way you can," Morunt said. "Or, at least, the way I think you can. I couldn't change my eye colour with all the food on this ship in my stomach. You're going to be able to do a lot of things I can't, but I wouldn't be in a hurry to tell anyone about that. I said you're stronger at detection, and you are, but you're stronger in other ways too. And you'll be better off if no one knows that, either."

Pendt was already keeping secrets, so it wasn't much of a stretch to add this one to the collection. She'd seen her cousin exposed and pliant; she was in no hurry to let anyone do the same thing to her.

# 6.

THE *HARLAND'S* BRIG WAS cool and dry and close enough to the engine room that the cyclers provided a constant, soothing hum. There was nothing to do there, which was part of what incarceration meant, but there was also *nothing to do*, which meant while you were in it, your time was your own.

Pendt's semi-regular confinement to the brig was not a new development. Before the fingernail incident, she had been considered her mother's to discipline. Now, if she was very lucky, she was locked in her room. It was barely big enough for her narrow cot and the cabinet that held her change of clothes and toiletries, but it was *hers*, and she could lock the door from the inside too.

The downside was that the air circulation was so poor, Pendt often woke gasping in the middle of the night, desperate for more oxygen. Her rank on the *Harland* didn't entitle her to any repair allotments, so she just had to bear it.

"A rat hole for the galley cat," said Kaeven. Lodia made him check the environmentals after the fourth time Pendt was found passed out in the hallway that led to the toilets, but he did a cursory job at best. "It's no better than you deserve."

Her brothers all lived in a bunkroom across the hallway from her closet. Lodia had a small room, though hers was much nicer than Pendt's, and then there was the toilet facility. There was no common area. If they wished to socialize, they did it in the mess or the crèche-turned-gym. Pendt rarely wished to socialize.

The lights in the galley were dim, only lighting the workspaces the minimal amount to assist with food preparation. Pendt had been released from confinement a few minutes before the pre-dinner shift began and told to report for duty. There was no doubt that this was still part of her punishment, though. At lunch, she had mistakenly licked her fingers after getting vege-matter on them instead of putting her hands in the calo-recycler. The cook had reported her, of course, and Lodia-the-Officer had ordered Pendt to the brig. Her presence now was at the behest of her aunt, who never missed the chance to remind Pendt what she was worth to the *Harland*.

Pendt's brothers sat on one side of the long Family table. Lodia sat at the foot and Pendt's cousins sat with their backs to the galley. The elder generation of cousins, who had no offspring, were at the other table. Pendt looked out at the sea of light brown to white-blond hair she could see through the galley cutaway, and then turned her attention back to the task. Her aunt meant for her to hear whatever was about to happen, but not see it. Her stomach rumbled very softly.

"Talbor," said Arkady.

Pendt's younger brother stood and saluted: "Yes, sir?"

"Today you are eight, and ready to learn your place on the *Harland*," Arkady said. "You will have to work extra hard to make up for your family's lack, but I know you will do better than your best."

Pendt didn't need to see the room to know how everyone would react. Lodia would stare straight ahead, unflinching. Her brothers would look at their plates, and then up at their aunt like hopeful children. Her cousins would smirk. Everyone else would pretend not to know what was going on. Pendt tallied rations, counting calories into allotments to be given out at the next meal.

"I will, Captain," Talbor said.

And now Talbor, born of a trade with a mining colony that had resulted in a single fertilized egg for each party at the table, officially outranked her. It was difficult to keep track of time on the *Harland*, but if Talbor was eight, then that meant Pendt herself was almost eighteen, and they must be getting close to Brannick Station. Pendt's hands shook, and she steadied them before the cook could notice. The last thing she needed was more trouble, even if the brig was basically a vacation from the torture of working around so many calories all the time, knowing what she could do with them, and not being permitted to eat them.

Pendt lifted up several trays and headed out to distribute them, starting with the captain and working her way down the ranks. As she made her runs past the table, Talbor used his Spark deck to shoot little flecks of electricity at her arms. She'd rolled up the sleeves of her jumpsuit while she worked—he wouldn't have dared damage *that*—and each contact burned her skin with little marks she'd never be allowed to heal. She did not give her brother the satisfaction of responding. She was used to discomfort.

"Stupid cat," Talbor said. "Can't even feel a Spark when you hand it to her on a platter."

The twins snickered quietly and Karderee smirked, but no one else at the table even acknowledged her existence. Arkady was almost done eating.

A larger spark hit the back of Pendt's hand, right in the webbing between her two smallest fingers, and she hissed, dropping the cutlery she was trying to pass out.

"Whoever heard of a clumsy cat," Talbor said. A shower of sparks headed her way. Pendt had had just about enough of him. "Maybe we should trade you for a real one, though you probably aren't worth as much as one of those."

Something that Pendt couldn't name steamed through her and overflowed. She set down the last of utensils and turned to face her little brother. An unholy calm descended on her, some level of self-preservation she didn't know she possessed. That, at least, stopped her from screaming at him.

"Well, when we get back to Alterra in twenty years, maybe we'll try to trade your twin for you," Pendt said. Everyone looked at her, but she didn't notice. "She's the one that got star-sense, though, so you're probably not worth enough to get her back."

There was dead quiet in the mess. Even the engine hum seemed to stop.

"What did you say?" said Arkady, colder than the void and ten times as merciless.

"My little sister, sir," Pendt said. She'd spent the resources, and now there was no going back. She had to keep going and hope for the best. "The one we left."

Arkady struck her with her tray. The empty dishes and cutlery went flying, but the metal rectangle made contact with the side of Pendt's head, and she went down hard.

This time, there was no blood. Pendt had caught the full force of the blow, but not from the corner of the tray. She'd have a bruise; it hurt like hell, but there was no blood. She tried to stand up, but she was dizzy, and it was hard to find her feet. She focused on talking instead. It never did to keep Arkady waiting when she'd asked a question.

"I didn't know," Pendt said, fighting back tears of pain and surprise. Crying would only make it worse. She struggled to her knees. "I wasn't even ten and I didn't understand what my magic could do. I just sense her difference in the æther. I didn't know *why* until Tanith got pregnant."

All eyes turned to Tanith, whose hands flew to her belly. The distraction gave Pendt enough time to get back on her feet, leaning heavily on the table as she did. Everyone leaned away from her and she clung to the surface to maintain her balance and clear her head.

"Is my baby—" Tanith was rounding now, a ball attached to the scrawny beanpole that was the rest of her body. She didn't look healthy or comfortable, but she never said anything about it.

"I don't know," Pendt said. Tanith choked on a sob. Pendt felt no pity for her cousin at all. The baby was fine. Pendt wasn't about to waste her time on another Harland that would grow up to make her life hell. "That's how I learned. I know what gene-sense feels like in a child because I remember it. I sensed something in my sister, but didn't know what it was. Lodia felt different from the baby she carried. I can't tell yours apart from you."

"Can you change it?" Arkady's voice had a tone of desperation to it that made Pendt's blood run cold. Her aunt never sounded desperate, and Pendt didn't know how to respond to the newness of it.

Everyone on the *Harland* knew that the ship needed a baby with star-sense. They couldn't go back for the one they'd given up, but now that they knew Pendt could identify a future child, there were all sorts of new possibilities. Possibilities were not the sort of thing you wanted in the hard certainty of space. Especially not when Pendt was the one exposing them.

"There aren't enough calories on the whole ship," Pendt said after pretending to think about it, like changing her own genes to be something else had never crossed her mind. "It wouldn't work, I'd die, and you'd all starve to death before we reached the next port, unless you ate—"

She stopped short of saying "the crew," but everyone in the galley froze. Arkady Harland was a hard woman to serve, and no one really believed she'd stoop to cannibalism, but no one had ever heard her sound like this before. There was no telling where she'd strike.

"When we get to Brannick Station, your life is going to change, girl," Arkady gritted out. "You best stay clear of me in the meantime, in case I forget how much you'll be worth someday and decide to airlock you anyway."

"Yes, Captain," Pendt said.

It was, technically, the first time anyone had ever chosen in her favour.

She didn't like it.

# 7.

**THESE WERE THE THINGS** Pendt Harland knew:

Family was everything, her ship was home, her aunt's authority was absolute, and as her birthday crept closer, she was descending into an endless abyss of bodily horror she was finally beginning to understand.

When her mother had been pregnant with Talbor, Pendt had been too young to understand. When her period started and her calories were increased, Pendt gained stronger awareness of her body and, though she didn't realize until Tanith's procedure, a similarly better awareness of the bodies that surrounded her.

Dr. Morunt had persuaded Arkady to let Pendt study medical texts in preparation for when Pendt would be old enough to hire out to other families and ships. At first, Pendt had been a reluctant student. She hadn't wanted to learn anything that would take her away from the only home she'd ever known, but as she read each new file, she realized the power in information. She wasn't just learning about how to diagnose and fix bodies, she was learning how they *worked*. The patterns she saw in people took on a clearer meaning. She knew their strengths and frailties now.

Arkady, for example, would have grown another three inches taller if she'd been given eight additional grams of protein a day when she was a teen. Lodia's bones were going to weaken over the next decade. It wouldn't be dangerous, but it would be uncomfortable. Two of her older cousins had XXY chromosomes. No one asked Pendt for any information and she didn't answer unasked questions, but she filed everything away for the future, in case it ever became something she could use.

Dr. Morunt was the most fascinating person to read the genes of, and Pendt did so even though she couldn't quite shake the feeling that she was intruding. Morunt read everyone else's genes all the time, after all, though she said she couldn't read as closely as Pendt could. That was how she calculated everyone's calorie allotment.

In the doctor's genes, Pendt could trace the pattern of the power they shared. The pathways of her magic were well-worn and comfortable, because Morunt used her magic all the time. If Pendt looked at herself, she could see that her magic was a wild tangle of unmapped space—no surprise, since she lacked almost all of Morunt's experience—but it was undoubtedly . . . bigger.

Tanith's growing foetus was Pendt's favourite object of study. The existence of the baby still terrified her, and Tanith's increasingly sallow skin and listless behaviour as the pregnancy progressed wasn't good for anyone, but the idea of the baby, the newness of it and the flexibility of its growth was irresistible.

She'd told Arkady that she couldn't change the baby's genes

without more calories than they had on the ship, and she had been telling the truth. But the child was growing, its genes making new decisions every moment of every day. Pendt couldn't force it into a new pattern, but she could watch as it built itself up from two cells into a person, and in watching, she learned how she could shape it, if she only had the calories to do so.

Arkady asked her frequently what she had learned, and Pendt always had a ready answer about some disease or a broken bone. She never lied; she was still too much a Harland for that. She knew better than to admit that she was starting to think her magic, though different, was more powerful than her aunt's.

She had also started to read non-medical texts in her studies. The library on the *Harland* was one big system, so it wasn't like she was going somewhere she wasn't allowed to be. As long as she was on time for her shifts in the galley, no one ever questioned her decision to read as much as possible. Her brothers didn't even make fun of her for it, largely because they didn't know how to.

She read history and stellar cartography, learning about the Stavenger Empire and the vast swaths of space they had once claimed to rule. She learned about the oglasa, which used to fill the void between the stars and were now reduced to a fraction of their former numbers. And she puzzled her way through legal documents until she fully understood how, with its dying gasps, the Stavengers had locked their subjects into place. Each station had a family, the way the *Harland* did, only locked to the family's DNA and controlled by the Y chromosome. It was an entirely new way of thinking for Pendt. On the *Harland*, girls were inherently more valuable, as they maintained custody of their children over any paternal claim. The ships wanted daughters and the stations wanted sons, though most of the people who lived and worked in less powerful positions didn't really care.

Pendt also came to understand that the Stavengers had done her a favour with at least one of their decrees. In order for a generation ship to maintain contracts with the stations and mining installations, they must be able to prove that they were not exploiting child labour. No one under the age of eighteen could be contracted into anything outside their own family. As soon as a person turned eighteen, the head of their family had all the rights to decide everything from their working situation to their living arrangements. Pendt knew that when Arkady made decisions about her, it would be for the *Harland*'s best interests, not anything so unimportant as Pendt's well-being. Tanith had shown her that. She was ten years older than Pendt, and an electro-mage too, and her body was not her own.

A chime sounded and Pendt closed the file on developmental psychology that she was reading. The concept was alien to her. The only things that developed on the *Harland* were skills to keep the ship going and sense to stay out of everyone's way. Encouraging a child by promoting its hobbies was entirely foreign. Pendt had needed the dictionary to learn what a hobby was.

The chime meant that it was time for the graveyard shift to start—the skeleton crew who maintained the engines and the *Harland*'s course while everyone else slept. Pendt needed to go to sleep too, or she would be too tired to work tomorrow, and might lose her reading privileges. The medical bay was dim and quiet, empty for now since everyone was well. Morunt went about her tasks with little chatter, as always. Pendt got ready to leave so that the doctor could seek her own bunk, but she seemed in no particular hurry this evening.

"I'm glad we're close to Brannick Station," Morunt said, absently putting the needles into the medical sterilization unit. "It's been a long couple of decades and I need to replace some things. I'll have to work on my requisition forms, but the captain is pleased with our ore haul, so I'm cautiously optimistic. Four more weeks."

Four weeks to Brannick Station, and Pendt's life would change, even though she didn't know all the details about how. Her birthday would fall around that time, and her aunt would contract her out. She might never see the *Harland* again. And to be perfectly honest, she wasn't entirely sure she wanted to.

Leaving the Family behind had once filled her with fear. Now, it was merely another wretched situation she probably couldn't avoid, only this time with people who bought her, and therefore probably appreciated her presence just a little bit. If she had been going somewhere new to cook and clean, or even to do Dr. Morunt's job, she might have welcomed the idea of a change, even if it was intimidating. But as Tanith's form reshaped itself around the new life she carried, Pendt understood that her future had always been her body. Her family would rent out her ability to grow healthy children. The idea of being reduced to that was bad enough. She knew how pregnancy wreaked havoc on the body, medically and from observation. She didn't want that to be her whole life. If they knew that she was pretty sure she could *design* children, or at least select their genetic progress with some deliberation, she'd never be free.

Dr. Morunt had given her a warning. She understood and appreciated it. She had four weeks. If she was ever going to anything, it would have to start now.

In the quiet of the medical bay, reading files she wrestled into understanding, Pendt Harland discovered that she knew more things now:

Family was everything; her ship was home; her aunt's authority was absolute; and as her birthday crept closer, her already limited freedoms became more and more curtailed.

Pendt looked down at her fingernails, and made a plan.

In the end, it was both ridiculously easy and impossibly hard. Pendt saved one gram of oglasa from her dinner portion every day for four weeks. It was all she could spare. Her body was already running close to the margin, operating at peak efficiency thanks to eighteen years of training. Any more than a gram per day, and her work would suffer. She might be caught.

She felt the loss of that gram every moment. Worse, she knew exactly where her hoard was, and that she could eat it at any time if she wanted to. It haunted her, and her dreams were full of giant fish that mocked her as they floated in the black of space. But she stayed strong. She was only going to get one chance at this, and there would be no going back. She did her best to put the growing pile of calories out of her mind.

The part that almost made her laugh was that the whole scheme was only possible because of circumstances *she* had caused. If she hadn't regrown her fingernail all those years ago, they never would have had to trade for more food at Alterra. They never would have

ended up with Talbor. Their food supplies would be endless protein packets, not the densely nutritious oglasa. She didn't even
have to wrap it or keep it somewhere cool. Oglasa didn't spoil.
She could have stored it next to the engine, and four weeks later,
it would still be edible.

The rest of her escape was fairly straightforward. Pendt had
witnessed several dockings now, and she knew how this one would
go. The *Harland* would make port, the engines would cut off, and
Arkady and Lodia would go aboard the Brannick Station. No
one else would leave the ship, no Harland, at least. But the doors
below, in the hold where the passengers had stayed and possibly
died during the extended years of the voyage, those doors would
open. And no Harland cared what or who went through them.

The hard seal on the door between the hold below and the rest
of the ship was her biggest obstacle. She found a plan of the ship
and located an airduct that passed from one part of the ship to the
other. It was very, very small, but so was Pendt. It wasn't like she'd
be carrying anything with her.

The day came when the *Harland* arrived at Brannick Station.
Everything went exactly as Pendt imagined, except the part where
she ate the twenty-eight grams of protein she'd been hoarding.
Nothing could have prepared her for the surge of power she felt
rush through her body as it dealt with so much excess for the first
time in her life.

When the engines cut, Pendt headed for the airduct. She had
picked the one in her mother's room because Lodia would be gone
and Tanith would be in the engine room, running maintenance.
No one would see the open duct until much later, hopefully until

after the *Harland* had already left. It was a tighter fit than she was expecting, but Pendt was very determined. Despite the skin it cost her, she shoved herself through the duct, and into the vent that would lead her to the other side of the seal.

The hold below was not what she had been expecting. After so many years of passenger freight, she thought it would be dirty and full of waste and garbage. Instead, it was pristine, so clean it would have met Dr. Morunt's sterilization protocols. Any evidence of human habitation had been scourged. Beds lined the walls, stacked three high. Almost a hundred people could have lived here, Pendt realized. She thought it was more like thirty. Nothing about it made sense, but Pendt had no time to wonder about it. She had to make it through the doors while they were open.

When she crossed the airlock, she found a large empty bay. Like the hold, it was almost too clean to imagine that a group of people had passed through it, but the clock was still ticking, and Pendt still had to move.

She crossed the bay and the doors opened automatically at her presence. A nondescript corridor waited for her on the other side. Pendt took a deep breath and crossed into the unknown.

# 8.

PENDT WASN'T USED TO the weight of this much hair. It pulled at her scalp and ghosted along her neck, and even though she'd done her best to make it grow straight, she hadn't known what to do with it when she had it. She wasn't exactly in style, but she hadn't known what style was when she started this, so there wasn't really anything she could do about it. Almost everyone she'd ever seen before had the same hair: short, blond, and eminently practical. It's one of the reasons she'd picked something more elaborate for her escape attempt, and she didn't regret it for a second, even if she had no idea what to do with it.

She also wasn't used to this much sound. The *Harland* was an old ship, but it was solid and well constructed, and it ran smoothly, thanks to generations of gifted engineers. The engines' hum could only be heard in certain parts of the ship, and the walls were enough to mute raised voices and all but the most disastrous of mechanical failures. Here, there were people everywhere, crushing through the corridors as they walked between the docking ports and the service area on the station. She'd never seen so many kinds of bodies. They came in all shapes and sizes, and it was hard not to stare at the un-*Harland*ness of them all.

Most were dressed in jumpsuits, though the colours of these varied widely, and most had the same short hair Pendt was used to seeing on the *Harland*. There were a few, though, who were different. The women wore clothing cut to highlight the shape of their bodies, and then men dressed with sharp lines and hard corners, as though they could change their shape with fabric. They were clearly not on their way to buy engine lubricant or barter for additional berth-space on the docking ring.

The station boasted any number of places where food, alcohol, and various entertainments were peddled, and Pendt imagined that it was to these places the interestingly dressed people were headed. Looking down at her plain jumpsuit, she realized that she would stick out if she followed them, and since sticking out was the last thing Pendt wished to do, she withdrew into a corner to consider her options.

She was not going back. She didn't care how she was dressed in comparison with everyone else. They would get her back on the *Harland* when she was dead, or they would drag her kicking and screaming. She had already crossed the line, hoarding her rations and expending them on her hair and nails. That would earn her the punishment to end all punishments. There was nothing else they could do to make it worse.

Her calculation had been very precise: enough change to look different, but enough saved that she could change herself back.

That was the first rule, and the one by which the *Harland* flew, only spending what a thing was worth, and never a fraction more. Food, oxygen, clothing, it didn't matter. She had only ever had exactly what she needed to survive. She could alter herself further, she had the calories for more æther work, but then she'd be stuck unless someone bought her a drink. Pendt did not like to rely on other people. Other people were usually awful.

Or, at least, her family was awful. Maybe here it would be different. She could smile and make conversation and hope for the best. Pendt wasn't used to hoping for much of anything at all, but, well, she had already come this far. She could go a little further.

She looked out at the crush of people walking past the little oasis she'd found in the corridor. They were all moving quickly, eyes forward, target acquired. No one was watching her. She could do whatever she wanted. So she closed her eyes, and reached inside.

The jumpsuit was made of plant fibre, harvested from the hydroponics bay and treated so that it was tear-proof and fire-retardant, but it was still a plant. She tightened the weave of it around her stomach, hips, and below her knees. It was nowhere near as eye-catching as the people she'd seen, but at least she no longer wore a shapeless bag. Next, she changed the colours: deeper green for the bottom half and lightening until the collar around her neck was white. She detached the sleeves and stuffed them into her bag; it went against her nature to discard things.

And then, using the last of her expendable calories, she added the slightest tinge of green to her newly darkened hair. It was ridiculous, a useless reason to put forth the effort, but she found she didn't care.

Pendt rejoined the crowd and followed the crush down to the level where the entertainments were. Down was an awkward concept for a space traveler. It was possible that she was traveling sideways and standing on the wall. Still, her mother had once told her that it was best to take advantage of direction while she had it. Pendt usually ignored most of her mother's advice, but this particular idea would probably prevent an existential crisis, and Pendt was all about preventing crises today.

Brannick Station thronged with people. They were loud and they had little respect for one another's personal space as they jostled through the wider colonnades of the station's public market area. Pendt knew from the blueprints she had stolen out of her brother's desk that the station had more than one public sector. This one was simply for the most itinerant travelers. If you wanted to stay, you needed to go up a few levels and submit an application. If you were rich, there was another level altogether.

Pendt put her hand on the wall and felt the quiet rumble of the structural integrity generators. They, like all the rest of the station's life support, were tied to the Brannicks, making them lord and master of everyone and everything on board. Pendt didn't imagine she would ever come to their attention. She had no lord or master now and didn't plan to ever again.

There were a few details to work out, of course. She would have to find a job and a place to live. She wanted to be independent of the *Harland*, and she had to bet on them leaving before they missed her. Once they were gone, there was no way her aunt would expend fuel to come back for a useless member of the crew. The neglect that had caused her so much pain as a child worked to her advantage now. She just needed to stay away long enough for them to go, and then she would be free. Surely someone on this station would have need of a cook. Pendt looked down at her bare arms. It didn't seem likely anyone would hire her for her sense of fashion.

The colonnade seethed around her and she moved along with the flow of the crowd. There were shops selling everything Pendt could imagine and more than a few things she couldn't. She'd never seen so many *things* before in her entire life. The *Harland*'s sharp austerity seemed colder than ever. This was probably the reason her aunt forbade anyone from leaving the ship the rare times the *Harland* was docked somewhere. Her aunt walked a hard line and forced everyone to walk it with her. She said it was necessary for space, which was dark and death and completely unforgiving, but Pendt was starting to wonder if maybe she just hoarded her family as much as she hoarded their calories.

Speaking of calories. It was time she found some, before she started to feel light-headed. She hadn't done this much æther work on purpose in her entire life, and she had no idea what the aftereffects were going to be.

She picked the establishment playing the loudest music, because it made her stomach rumble with something other than hunger, and she found that she liked the sensation quite a bit. She observed, circling the dance floor like a cat, as people at tables drank brightly coloured concoctions that smoked or bubbled or frothed, or sometimes did all three at once. Placed along the bar at regular intervals were tiny dishes filled with round tabs that Pendt thought might be edible. Her suspicions were confirmed when she saw a woman with spacer-short hair and a bright red bodysuit take a handful of them, and eat them all at once.

Pendt's mouth watered. She didn't even care what they tasted like. She had never seen anyone eat anything so carelessly, ever. Even when her brothers tormented her by flaunting their larger portions of food in her face, there was a sense of desperation, of gratefulness, to their behaviour. To eat and not care who was watching or how much you chewed or how many calories were left for others was a dream. Brannick Station was some kind of paradise.

Pendt slid up to the end of the bar, hoping to avoid the server's notice for as long as possible, and helped herself to one of the tabs. It was salty, but more than edible, and Pendt took a handful to put in her pockets in case the servers chased her out when they realized she didn't have any money. These would give her enough calories to hold on until she found a more reliable source. A little voice whispered that she could change back, if she wanted. That it wasn't too late, and she could go home, but she didn't listen. Home was behind her now. She was never going back to the *Harland* again. She ate four more of the tabs in a single mouthful, breaking them with her teeth and dragging the sharp edges along her tongue.

She was so focused on the little cup and the balls that she didn't notice the two figures that came to sit beside her until they were perched on the stools. They didn't flank her, so she didn't panic entirely, but they definitely noticed her, and Pendt didn't like what followed when people noticed her, particularly when she was eating. They were between her and the main exit, but she thought that she could lose them on the dance floor, if she needed to. She was smaller than they were, and had spent a lot of time moving through small spaces. She took a quick glance sideways to get a better look at them.

One of the figures had an open face—the sort of mark that her aunt liked to trade with—and was already smiling, half lost in the music. It was striking, to see someone so relaxed. Pendt didn't think she had ever been that comfortable in her life, let alone in a crowd. A part of her ached, wondering what her life would have been like if she hadn't always been so afraid. She was going to change that now too.

The other boy was all lines and angles, his nose like the prow of a grounding-ship and his face shaped to cut through atmosphere with no resistance. He had the face of someone who was listened to, but unlike her brothers, he didn't seem made cruel by it. Neither of them looked to be much older than Pendt's seventeen years, and she hadn't made herself look older when she changed, so maybe they just thought she would be good company. For some reason.

The first boy was looking straight at her, the way her aunt did when she was about to administer a judgement. Pendt was no stranger to direct confrontation; it just always went badly for her. She braced herself for something terrible, but when the second boy spoke, his words held none of the venom she was so used to taking.

"Now tell me," he drawled, helping himself to the tabs Pendt had left in the cup, "what's a girl like you doing in a place like this?"

# PART TWO

"HIGH, HIGH HOPES
FOR A LIVING"

A s dying breaths go, the Stavenger Empire had a good one. They made sure they didn't go into the dark alone. Unwilling to cede power, even in death, the Stavengers took a large portion of the galaxy with them when they went, and made life challenging for all those who remained.

The empire used up the last of their grain-mages by making æther locks. Each station was locked to the genetic code of the station's ruling family and controlled by the Y chromosome. If either code or chromosome was ever absent from the station, all functions ceased. It wasn't just that the Nets and Wells wouldn't work, the lights and the air recyclers and the heaters would cease to function too. To leave a station un-ruled was to kill it. The rebel leaders could no longer command from the front, and their sons' every breath was the future of the station's entire population.

The stations had been almost entirely united. The leaders of each family rallied their people to battle, and the people were willing to fight for them. No one could have anticipated the deterioration of the æther, and even after magic became unreliable, no one imagined the Stavengers would sacrifice so much for control they had already lost.

Records were essentially unobtainable, given the distance and political situation, but scholars on Katla Station estimated that more than a thousand gene-mages, called grain-mages by the Stavengers, would have been needed to make the gene-locks. Part of this was because it was a huge and intricate piece of magic. The other part was that they had to do it simultaneously for six different targets: Brannick, Enragon, Katla, Skúvoy, Hoy, Ninienne.

In the space of a few breaths, thousands died and each station became irrevocably locked to its ruling family. The full extent of this was not understood until the emergency messages from Enragon reached the other stations. The entire ruling line had been leading the rebellion from the front. When the lock went into operation and there was no Y chromosome to operate it, the entire station had instantly gone dark. Everyone who lived there died as soon as the oxygen reserves ran out, if they didn't freeze to death first. No one had been to check.

And no one could, either. The Nets were part of the lock too, and without an Enragon to activate the Net on the station (or an Enragon to make the jump himself and turn it on automatically), the station was unreachable except by old-fashioned sublight travel, and that was going to take some time.

Time was something the dying rebellion did not have. Now that they were isolated from one another, it was difficult to organize anything. Furthermore, the gene-lock made it so that the inhabitants of the stations lived in fear of their rulers leaving. No one wanted to die gasping in the cold dark of space, after all. To maintain order, the stations reorganized so that the right chromosomes were always in residence, ensuring the lights stayed on and station operations could continue, albeit on a smaller scale.

The Stavenger forces were also recalled. They took male hostages from each family—except the extinct Enragons—and returned to their home solar system to rebuild. There was always a threat hanging then, that someday the Net would activate and a Stavenger army would be let in by the station's own, however unwillingly. It also limited the number of available cousins. Thus the stations and the remnants of the empire reached some tentative, unhappy peace while the æther healed.

Generations later, just after Fisher and Ned Brannick turned eighteen, their uncle was diagnosed with a terminal liver condition. They had never met the man, but his illness impacted their lives tremendously: He was the family hostage, and now he was dying. The empire was merciless, demanding that a Brannick be sent to replace the one they were losing. Fisher couldn't go himself, and Catrin Brannick refused to let her other son be taken either. In the end, she and her husband, Ned the Elder, went, he to provide the hostaged genes and she because she wouldn't be separated from him.

This left Brannick Station in the control of Ned, called Brannick the Younger since he and his father shared a name. Though he had been raised in anticipation of this day, Ned was not entirely prepared for it. Fortunately, he had his brother, and the two of them worked together to keep everyone on their station alive. Ships came in and ships went out, occasionally the Net was required, and as long as no one looked too closely, it seemed like everything was fine.

Ned and Fisher had dreams, of course. Imagined futures where they did other things and served themselves instead of a station full of dependents. They were too well trained to do anything but quietly make the occasional pointless wish that things were different. They had jobs to do and people who relied on them, and they would do their duty, as every Brannick had always done.

The space station gene-locks were a method of control. The limits they placed on travel were a feature, not a bug. The best way to quell a rebellion is through immobilization. If you shut down a movement, the kinetic energy builds up until it explodes, and then your problem is over.

More or less.

# 9.

## BRANNICK STATION

**ABSOLUTELY NONE OF THIS** was Fisher's fault. There was no way it could be. Generations of despotic rule by a far-off empire literally ensured it. And yet, here was Fisher: at fault.

The problem with coordinating the sublight ships arriving at Brannick Station was that nothing happened for long stretches of time and then everything happened all at once. There hadn't been a shipment from the mine run in three years, and now two ships were due to arrive at the same time. Brannick Station was in good shape, but not good enough to deal with the off-loading of two shipments' worth of ore at the same time.

Fisher's teeth ground together as the docking schedule flashed across the screen and refused to change of its own accord. There was nothing for it: He would have to inform the overseers that they were going to need emergency overtime to get the job done. At least the station could still afford to pay fair wages. The problem was that there were fewer people around to do the work.

Ned swung into the seat behind him, thirty minutes late for

the start of the duty shift as unavoidably as usual. This, Fisher did not hold against him. Ned could barely cross a hallway these days without two dozen station residents shouting for him. The perils of being the Brannick; a burden that Fisher would never share, even though they both carried the name. Getting from their quarters all the way to Brannick Station's main working offices was something of a challenge.

"Good morning," Fisher said. "We have a labour shortage."

"Tell me something I don't know," Ned replied. The mug he held was steaming. Fisher could only hope it wasn't too packed with artificial stimulants.

"We're about to feel the pinch again," Fisher continued. "We've got two mine-run ships coming in within, as far as I can tell, thirty-six hours of each other."

"Names?" Ned leaned forward, his eyes suddenly bright again as his focus narrowed. It was a dangerous look.

"The *Harland* and the *Cleland*," Fisher said, on alert. "You recognize the names of ships now?"

It wasn't an ill-meant jab. Ned really was trying, and there were a lot of ship names to remember. Fisher would rather Ned remember station operations. He could ask the database for anything outside of that.

"I recognize the ones I'm helping coordinate," Ned said with nothing even remotely resembling subtlety.

Fisher resisted the urge to vent all atmosphere from the room.

"Which ship is full of rebels?" Fisher called up the manifest for both ships. Whoever had forged the records had done an amazing job. Even knowing what to look for, Fisher couldn't tell which was the fake.

"The *Cleland*," Ned said. "You're not too angry?"

"I would have appreciated a bit more time to work on a cover-up," Fisher admitted. "I hadn't told the foreman about the overtime yet, but it was the next thing on my list."

"I'm sorry, Fisher," Ned said. "I did mean to tell you."

Fisher took a long look at the boy in the other chair. There were dark circles under his eyes. Ned was exhausted and there was very little Fisher could do to help.

The same rules that kept Fisher from running operations on Brannick Station kept Ned locked into them. Though they were twins and Fisher was thirty-eight minutes older, Ned had the necessary chromosomes for the station's gene-lock, and that meant he had become the Brannick when their parents had been called away by the Hegemony. It was antiquated and stupid, but there wasn't anything they could do about it.

So Fisher helped out, coordinating shipments and keeping the station operating as much as was possible given the need for Ned's gene-lock to keep the life-support systems running. And Ned was trapped, far away from the front lines of a war he was desperate to take part in, and had to settle for smuggling rebel miners through the station's Well to send them to the front.

"You've arranged for a Net?" It was paranoia, but it was always something worth confirming.

"The shipment is expected," Ned replied. He had just enough star-sense to be absolutely terrified at the idea of being marooned in deep space. "They'll be here for six hours while they pretend to off-load ore, and then they'll jump."

"Six hours isn't a lot of time," Fisher said. He knew the limits of Brannick's people as well as their equipment: He could feel it in the sparks.

"Tell the *Harland* you rushed it to accommodate them," Ned suggested. He took a drink. "Our more reliable merchants always get preference, even when they don't make berth first."

"I never would have thought of that," Fisher admitted. He made a note in the file.

"My charm lends itself to conspiracy," Ned said, waggling his eyebrows. "Yours just makes people want to do their best for you. We're basically unstoppable, and the longer the Hegemony doesn't know that, the better."

Their parents had been a good team too. Ned Brannick the Elder, husband of Catrin, had held the station to higher standards of operating than a Brannick had done in decades. They were efficient, respected, and the Hegemony had summoned them through the Well eight months ago to be the new genetic hostage. With Ned the Younger to hold the gene-lock, they had no excuse to refuse, and so they had gone.

It took a few days to get from Brannick Station to the Stavenger system, even if you didn't pause at the other stations along the way. Centuries ago, the ruling class of Stavenger's main planet had built the stations as a way to reach the Maritech system. Having more or less expanded as much as they could in their own solar range, they wanted to plunder someone else's. The stations—and more important: the Wells—allowed them to ricochet through the vast empty blackness between the two systems. Unfortunately, for them, the inhabitants of the Maritech planets had been less than welcoming, and had driven them back out into space.

The original Stavenger Empire was long gone, fractured into pieces that the Hegemony tried to keep in line, but the stations remained. They were mostly a dead end, with Brannick Station at the end of the line. A few explorers came to use the Brannick Well, but no one knew if the Maritech Net was still intact, and the lack of returning travelers seemed to indicate it wasn't. If a ship used a Well and missed the Net, there wasn't enough rocket fuel in the galaxy to slow the ship down before the crew ran out of food. Fisher's parents would have had adequate supplies and a known route through the Wells, but none of them had expected a happy ending when the family separated. Either they would never see each other again, or their return would herald an invasion.

The burden fell hardest on Ned, who was responsible for keeping the station alive. Fisher knew he wanted revenge, wanted to join the fight that had been picking up speed since they'd been born, but until there was another Brannick on the station with the right chromosomes, there was nothing either of them could do.

So they compromised. Fisher tried to keep their parents' hard work from falling apart and Ned supported the rebellion in whatever way he could. It wasn't enough for either of them, and it wouldn't be enough for Brannick Station in the long run, but right now it was all they had. And while they held the line, Brannick Station bled out slowly: losing loyal people to the front and resources to the various criminals who moved in to take their places.

The Stavenger Empire had gone to Maritech for resources

and failed to establish a foothold when they invaded, but the space around the stations wasn't as empty as they'd first thought. There were asteroids to mine and gasses to trap. Moreover, there were creatures in the void, drawn to the wells, and those creatures were a resource too. As long as there was something to exploit, the stations were worth holding on to. And as long as there had been stations, they had been trying to break free.

This was the true cruelty of the Hegemony's gene-lock. It affected only one or two people directly, but it gave those few incredible power over the lives of thousands, and some were not suited to bear that weight. The cost of open rebellion was simply too high. The network of Wells wasn't much, in the face of the Hegemony's power, but it was absolutely necessary for the survival of the stations, and it couldn't afford to lose another link. The whole station hung on Ned's every inhalation, and Fisher both envied and pitied him for it. It was a balance. A stalemate. And they both did the best they could, refusing to let the Hegemony push them apart.

Stalemates were never good for people like Ned Brannick. Which meant they weren't good for people like Fisher Brannick either, because for good or ill, they came as a pair. Ned was too smart to risk the station in an open fight, especially with the open wound that was their missing parents, but Fisher wasn't sure how much longer Ned would be able to control himself, and if the station would be ready for whatever Ned tried.

So: mining ships. Some with ore, some with rebels. A middle ground that left neither of them entirely pleased, but still let them feel like they were doing something about their situation. A light on Fisher's terminal began to blink.

"Please be the *Cleland*," Ned whispered.

"It is," Fisher told him. "They'll be here in four hours and they say the *Harland* is right behind them."

"Dammit," Ned said.

"I can stall for six hours," Fisher promised. "If we have to, we can actually break something."

"Give them a food bonus," Ned suggested. "We've had a good season in hydroponics, and those merchant ships always run tight on calories."

Ned's sense of the stars was about as strong as Fisher's sense of electronics: Enough to know there was more out there, but it still required the occasional caloric bump if they tried anything. A merchant ship ran on more than manual labour, and Ned was right. They always needed more food.

"That should make them happier about the wait," Fisher said. "I'll grant them full access to the station as well."

"Spacers never come aboard," Ned pointed out. "It's against their religion or something."

Fisher only shrugged. "Charm, remember? Granting access they won't use literally costs us nothing, but it makes you look good. I'll open the hatches and arrange for a moderate decon."

"I miss Mum and Dad," Ned said. It seemed like a bit of a non sequitur, but Fisher understood what he meant. It was a lot to keep track of, and only eight months of practice made them feel like they were just keeping enough oxygen in the tank. An emergency could blow them sideways.

"We have each other," Fisher said, and began to run the pre-clearance so that the approaching ships could land.

# 10.

THE *CLELAND* MADE BERTH just as the station's darklight shift took over. It couldn't have been better if Ned had planned it, but Fisher knew they'd been lucky. Well-ships came in on schedule, ready for the Net the instant they predicted. Sublight ships arrived whenever they arrived. Any manner of things could go wrong in space, and a rocket misfire at any point in the trip could speed up or slow down a ship as the star-sense-led captains wrestled their vessels along a true course.

"You can't go down and help," Fisher said as Ned cleared the last docking regulations with his gene-print and prepared to leave the office.

"Why not?" Ned asked, already half out of his chair. "I'm in charge."

"You never off-load mining ships," Fisher pointed out. "It has to be the same as any other *especially* because this ship is not the same as any other."

Ned made a face. It made him look younger, but Fisher knew this was not the time to point that out.

"Fine," Ned grumbled, slumping back. "You can go down, though. You do this sort of thing all the time."

"I do," Fisher admitted. "Is there anything I should be on the lookout for?"

"I have no idea," Ned said. "I just coordinated their arrival here and made sure they'll be able to leave through the Well."

He sounded so morose about it that Fisher felt a swell of pity. Ned had been raised to lead, but not so soon, and losing their parents on top of all the new responsibilities was not going well for either of them. At least no one had ever really needed Fisher.

"I know you want to do more," Fisher said. He put a hand on his brother's shoulder and Ned reached up to squeeze it. "But you are literally the only person in the galaxy who can do *this*."

Ned sat up a bit straighter at his terminal. They never talked about Fisher's genetics, having decided years before that they'd arrived on Brannick Station as twins for a reason: They were a pair. They each filled in for the other where they could and made sure the Hegemony didn't understand how reliant they were on each other.

"All right," Ned said. "Go check on our new mine transfers. Make sure they're equipped for their jump to Katla."

Fisher nodded and left the office. There was no point in asking who the contact on Katla Station was. Ned probably didn't know, and it was much safer for everyone if Fisher didn't. Someday, Fisher reflected, they were going to have to sit down and talk about everything they ran separately from each other, but there was no place on the station that was entirely secure. The control office was swept, of course, but if they spent all their time there, it would look equally suspicious.

Main operations was running at half staff for the dark-light shift. Fisher nodded to the officers on duty. They were all Brannick-born, and Ned was reasonably sure they were loyal, but Fisher maintained some distance from them all the same. Not having to be the Brannick people liked had its advantages, and Fisher enjoyed the privacy.

Fisher took the lift down, bypassing the colonnade entirely. At this time, the daylight shift would be arriving in the bars and restaurants, and the shops would be crammed full of people on their way back to their apartments. The lift cruised through the habitation levels, changing direction to accommodate for the less-than-logical station layout.

Brannick Station was the last part of the relay to be constructed. The Stavenger Empire hadn't ever intended for the relays to be long-term habitation centres. They'd thought of them as mere layover stations to the Maritech system. By the time they built Brannick, they had it down to an art. The oldest part of the station was blocky and graceless; a huge cylinder of mooring points supported by a refinery, power-generation facility, and carbon scrubbers. As the station expanded to include areas for people to actually live, separate power sources had been built, allowing the sections of the station to function independently. This was theoretically for safety, but it opened up opportunities as well.

Fisher's lift was for station personnel only, and Ned has used his override codes to make sure Fisher's trip was not interrupted, so it didn't take too long to arrive in the docking area. Fisher went over to the *Cleland*'s off-loading area, and waited until someone who looked like they were in a place of authority showed up.

"Excuse me?" Fisher said to the woman who seemed to be telling everyone else what to do. "I'm Fisher Brannick, station operations. Do you have everything you need?"

The woman looked at Fisher in a measuring sort of way, probably trying to figure out how much she could trust anyone on Brannick Station. She was short and her skin had a golden glow to it that wasn't common in a spacer. Skin tended to wash out in the void. She was either someone who spent most of her time stationside or she had an amazing skincare regimen. Fisher's face was open, if neutral, and the woman relaxed a bit after a few seconds.

"My name is Choria," she said. She gave no further identification. "And we have everything we require, thank you."

Fisher took a moment to look over the ship's manifest and made sure not to smile when the rebels' plan became clear. It was fairly simple, all told, but it would be enough. Fisher drew on the mantle that Ned wore sometimes to give orders. It made speaking in public a bit easier.

"I'm sorry to tell you that our station is not currently equipped to take on the volume of oglasa you have on board," Fisher said calmly. "We are primarily an ore-processing station."

"Yes," Choria said. "I am aware. We had planned to take the oglasa on to Katla Station, if we can reach some agreement for use of the Well."

That was smooth. The station relays had run on oglasa for centuries, but Brannick had never been the centre of operations for calorie extraction from them. They were fish—as much as anything could be a fish in deep space—and had been a primary food source for all space-going vessels until the stock was depleted from overharvesting. Now there were strict rules about collecting and transporting anything related to the oglasa harvest, and Brannick Station mostly stayed out of it by virtue of not having been involved in the first place. Sending the catch through the relay to Katla was the perfect excuse.

"I am sure we can reach some sort of arrangement," Fisher said. "We have another ore ship coming in behind you, so I am sure my brother will want to send you on your way as speedily as possible."

Choria smiled, her eyes brightening as if she and Fisher had shared a joke. In a way, they did. Everything had worked out perfectly for both of them.

"I appreciate that," Choria said. "Please convey my greetings to Brannick the Younger and tell him I look forward to working with him again."

She held out her hand for him to shake, and Fisher was not entirely surprised when a small datacrystal was pressed against his palm. The rebels had to keep in contact somehow. He would give it to Ned to decrypt, since it was probably for him anyway.

Fisher nodded, slid the crystal into one of his many pockets, and left the captain to her work.

Operations on the dock level was run out of a much tinier office than the one Fisher usually worked from, but it had its advantages. There was so much electrical interference from the power generator and refinery that covert surveillance was next to impossible. There were the station's cameras, of course, and anyone with half a spark could tap into them, but they were used to Fisher's advantage most of the time because he controlled where they were pointed.

Fisher watched as the *Cleland* off-loaded the small amount of ore it had brought as an excuse to travel, knowing that Ned was doing the same thing from his own terminal, and itching to be down here himself. The work went without a hitch, which was good because the tiny dot indicating the *Harland* was beeping with increased insistence as that ship drew near. After four hours, Fisher's comm link chimed.

"Brannick," Fisher said, not bothering to specify which one.

"This is the *Cleland*," Choria's voice sounded. "We have finished here, and would like to request passage though the Brannick Well."

"Patching you through to the gene-lock," Fisher said, and began to work on the pre-launch sequence. It wasn't like Ned was going to say no.

"Ned Brannick, live," Ned said through the comm. "My report shows that you have bartered twenty-five percent of your oglasa processing fee in return for passage. I accept. Please stand by while I coordinate with Katla Station."

Brannick Station could activate the Well, but the corresponding gene-lock on Katla was needed to set up the Net there before the *Cleland* could go anywhere, or the *Cleland* would literally never stop *going*. Katla had a few celestial surprises near its Net that made it necessary to be very precise with regard to timing. It usually took about five minutes to set up, but Fisher wasn't sure what time it was on Katla right now. If they had to wake up the station commander, it could take longer.

"Katla is ready for you, *Cleland*," Ned said, exactly five minutes later. "You are cleared to go in fifteen minutes. Activating your chronometer now."

Fifteen minutes was plenty of time for the *Cleland* to get itself into position. Choria hadn't asked for help, which meant her own star-sense was enough to calculate the angle she would need to hit the Well at in order to make the jump. It was good to know Fisher wasn't sending the ship out blind. Direction was complicated enough in space.

Fisher left the office and went to a viewing station. The Well wasn't activated so often that anyone could get tired of looking at it. Up on the colonnade, people were probably pressed against the ports, no matter how drunk they were. Fisher was glad of the relative quiet, because that made it easier to hear the hum of the Well kicking up.

Wells were mostly natural phenomena but bound in place for use by the Stavenger builders all those generations ago. They could be activated by anyone with power, originally, but now they were locked to the genetic inheritors of each station. This was how the Hegemony controlled the stars, even as those they controlled tried to rebel against them. Only Ned could bring the Brannick Well to life. Only Ned could catch incoming ships in the Net.

Fisher felt Ned's power stretch out from the station. Just the barest amount was needed to activate the Well, magnified through the conduits that connected the station to the universe. Then, just as the hum reached a volume where it started to hurt, the power surged and the Well flared up.

"This is the *Cleland*, heading out," said Choria. Her voice was elated through the comm, and Fisher couldn't blame her. The Well was beautiful, and her scheme had succeeded.

"Good sailing, *Cleland*," said Ned.

"Good sailing," Fisher echoed.

The chronometer counted down the last few seconds. Then the *Cleland*'s engines glowed as Choria slammed them into the Well at the angle she'd need. There was a surge of power—everyone on the station with any sense of anything would feel it—and then the *Cleland* streaked rainbow across the blackness of space and disappeared into æther.

"That never gets old," Ned said.

"No," Fisher agreed. The schedule indicated that they had two hours before the *Harland* arrived. "You should take a nap, if you can. We'll need you."

"We'll need you too," Ned said. "But I suppose you're going to take a stimulant instead."

"I am," Fisher said. "I'll sleep when the *Harland* is done."

"You'd better," Ned said, and the comm went quiet.

The screens changed to show the interior of the ore-processing facility as Fisher coordinated the work that needed to be done before the next shipment arrived. Fisher went to the calorie dispenser and requested something to stay awake. It didn't taste very good, but it would do the job, and that meant Fisher could too.

# 11.

NED RETURNED FIFTEEN MINUTES before the *Harland* was due, which meant he couldn't have gotten very much sleep. He looked better, though, and he wasn't drinking a stimulant this time, so Fisher counted it as a win. It was nearing midnight on the station's chronometer, the darklight shift half over. The restaurants and shops on the colonnade were long closed, but a few bars would still be open. Fisher didn't frequent any of them, but he did read the health inspection reports, so he knew what amenities the station had to offer.

"This ship has been out there for twenty years," Ned said, reading the screen in front of him. "The last time it was here, we weren't even born yet."

"How old is that ship?" Fisher asked. The newer ships could make the mining run in five years. Two decades meant the ship was practically ancient, and probably huge.

"It's old," Ned said. "It'll have to dock on the lower half of the ring."

That made unloading slightly more complicated, but there was nothing for it. That was the only place they could put a ship of that size. What they lacked in speed, they made up for in hauling capacity.

"Get a load of this thing." Ned was now looking at a technical readout of the ship. "Most of it is engine and cargo space. There's like four rooms. I would go absolutely insane."

Ned did not take well to staying in one place, which wasn't exactly a quality one looked for in the person who was locked into Brannick Station by his genetics, but at least the station was gigantic and there was plenty to do.

"Only the captain and first officer are scheduled to come on board," Fisher said. "They're not even helping unload. It's going to be all on our end."

Ned shuddered.

The boys watched as the docking procedures were completed and the airlocks regulated. As expected, only one crew airlock cycled for use, along with the main and auxiliary holds.

"There's nothing in the second hold," Fisher reported, skimming the official register. "They're just opening up to maximize air recycling. I'm going to switch the cameras to run maintenance."

"That's fair enough," Ned said. "And also handy, since that's where we should have unloaded the *Cleland*, so they might think it was weird if the hold was empty when they know there was a ship in front of them."

"Everything is working out very nice for you," Fisher said sarcastically. "I didn't nearly have a heart attack or anything."

Ned didn't reply.

"Do you want to go oversee the unloading?" Fisher offered an olive branch. "If you start doing it on regular shipments, you can do it when your friends come in as well."

Ned brightened. He was out of his chair and heading for the door before Fisher could draw breath. It was something, at least.

Fisher watched on the monitors as the ship was unloaded. It was strange not to have anyone get off and help or supervise or go get a drink on the colonnade. Instead, the Brannick team removed enormous crates of semi-processed ore from the hold of the *Harland*, stacking them in the cavernous loading bay until they figured out what was going where. A requisition list popped up on Fisher's screen, mostly medical supplies and food. He sent it on to the quartermaster to be filled. Everything seemed to be going smoothly. Fisher even saw Ned shaking hands with a tall woman he assumed was the captain. She didn't look particularly thrilled about it.

A flicker of movement caught his eye. All the cameras in the other loading bay were maintenance cycling through one monitor since there wasn't anything going on there right now. Or at least, there wasn't supposed to be anything going on there right now. Fisher turned away from his brother's image, and brought up the secondary cameras on more screens until he found what he was looking for.

A small figure dropped out of the *Harland* and made her way across the empty floor. It had been scrubbed after the *Cleland* had departed, partly as procedure and partly to destroy evidence, so there wasn't really anything for her to hide behind as she crossed the deck. The door opened for her automatically, and she seemed to hesitate before crossing the threshold, as if it was the most important step she'd ever take.

With a flash of insight, Fisher realized that it probably *was* the most important step she'd ever taken. She didn't look older than he was, which meant she had been born on the *Harland* and had probably never stepped foot anywhere else. Fisher wondered whether it was curiosity or desperation that drove her.

The girl stepped into the hallway and Fisher looked for the next footage of her. By the time he tracked her down, she had changed. Her hair was longer and darker, and her jumpsuit was a different colour. He watched while she changed its shape, making the suit more form-fitting and less of a coverall. For a moment, he wondered if he'd had too many stimulants, but then it struck him. She must be a gene-mage. And not just any gene-mage, either. There were four doctors on Brannick who could read a person's genes with varying ability, but none who could *change*.

He sent a signal to Ned, hoping his brother would return to the office right away. They had to talk before the girl went back to the *Harland*. But Ned was busy helping move crates—of all the times to decide to start doing that!—and didn't notice the message. Fisher watched onscreen as the girl went farther into the station. She didn't seem to be looking for anything in particular, but neither was she wandering at random. She stuck to crowds, like she was hiding or trying to blend in. She followed the movement of the masses, heading past the shopfronts until she reached one of the most notorious bars on the station. She paused for a moment, and then ducked inside.

On the loading dock, the crates were almost all in place. The *Harland*'s captain had already sent the first officer back to the ship. Ned was directing the placement of the last few crates. It occurred to Fisher that he could stall the requisitions, but no sooner had the idea come to him than the quartermaster arrived with everything ready to go. Usually, Fisher was very proud of the station's efficiency, but at the moment, it was causing a small dilemma.

He kept half an eye on the feed that monitored the bar. She hadn't left yet. She had to know how tight the timing was. Her captain probably bragged about how little time they spent in port. If she was going to get back, she was going to have to get moving.

. . . If she *wanted* to get back. She'd snuck out and changed her physical appearance. She didn't have anything with her, but maybe she hadn't been able to bring her possessions. If this was an escape, it was pretty dire, but it wasn't a half-bad attempt. There was always work available on Brannick. And she was a gene-mage. They would be beyond lucky to have her. Which of course meant her captain must also want her. Fisher couldn't see the whole picture yet, and he was sure he was missing something important.

He watched helplessly while the *Harland*'s captain went back onto the ship and began the exit procedures. They weren't using the Well, so they didn't need Ned or any calculations or clearance. They'd just let operations know when they wanted the clamps released. Both of the cargo-hold doors were closing, sealing against the vacuum of space.

Ned came back into the office, whistling cheerfully.

"They weren't so bad," he said. "In a hurry because they're meeting up with someone in a month for a contract and they have to control the engine burn or something, but aside from that, they weren't as standoffish as I was expecting."

"Someone got off their ship," Fisher said tightly.

"Yes, I talked to the captain and the first officer," Ned said.

"No, through the lower hold," Fisher said. "A girl."

"What?" Ned's attention snapped to the monitor Fisher was using. "Why didn't you tell me?"

"I tried!" Fisher said. "You didn't answer me."

"Why did you send it privately?" Ned asked. "You could have called the bay directly."

"She's a gene-mage," Fisher said. "I watched her grow her hair twelve inches and change its colour. She changed her outfit too. And she snuck out, Ned. I think she might be escaping."

"From what?" Ned said.

"I don't know," Fisher said. "Maybe she doesn't like space travel. But she's in a bar on the colonnade, and I think you should go talk to her."

"Why?" Ned said. "She can find a job if she talks to the quartermaster. There are signs posted everywhere."

"She's a *gene-mage*, Ned." Fisher resisted the urge to shake him by his shoulders. "Not like our doctors. She can *alter* things."

It hung there for a moment between them, and then understanding dawned in Ned's eyes.

"You're out of your mind," Ned said, leaning back in his chair.

"She ran away," Fisher repeated.

"Maybe she murdered everyone else on the ship while the captain was in the hold," Ned said.

"I think we should go talk to her," Fisher said.

"Oh, it's *we* now?" Ned said. He winced, immediately regretting what he'd said. "I'm sorry, Fisher. It's always both of us. I know that. I just . . . did not imagine meeting girls this way, you know?"

Fisher managed not to roll his eyes, but it was a near thing. In space, the *Harland*'s engine fired. It would take a month of controlled burning to bring it back to Brannick now, and it would use up all the fuel in its reserves. Having just unloaded cargo, they would never be able to afford to refuel. Maybe this escape attempt wasn't so morbid after all. Or maybe this girl was like Fisher, and things just worked out for her. But she was still running from people who couldn't come back for her.

It didn't matter. They were all here, and they had an opportunity, the three of them, even if they didn't know each other yet.

"Should I brush my teeth?" Ned asked. He checked his reflection.

"Ned, you make business deals with total strangers all the time," Fisher said.

"I think my hair looks too spiky."

"I will murder you."

"Can I see a clearer picture of her?" Ned asked. Fisher raised an eyebrow. "So I recognize her at the bar, jerk."

Fisher cued up the camera and found a good image of the girl's face. She was pale, but not entirely unattractive. Her eyes didn't suit her face, which was a strange thing to think about a person, but he couldn't shake the thought once it occurred.

"Okay, I'm ready," Ned said. He did not sound ready, but he did sound determined. "Let's shut down operations for the night and go to the bar."

It was almost that easy. It took Ned half an hour to extract himself since they had to walk out the main doors to get to the colonnade and people had questions for him. After that, it was only a few more minutes to walk to the bar. This late, no civilians were going to pester the Brannick.

They heard the music before the rounded the corner. The bass was pumping, making Fisher's ears throb before they even got inside. He didn't actually mind the song, just the volume at which it was pounding through his skull. He spotted the girl quickly enough, pulling on Ned's sleeve to get him moving in the right direction. She was sitting at the bar, eating the little nuts that the bartenders put out to make everyone thirsty.

For the rest of his life, Fisher could never think about what happened next without dissolving into uncontrollable laughter. He watched as his brother made his way across the floor, moving like a person who commanded a space station, only to lean against the bar and say the worst possible thing.

"Now tell me," he said, with all the grace of unevenly packed ore crate, "what's a girl like you doing in a place like this?"

# 12.

PENDT MANAGED NOT TO punch him, but only just. The other boy burst out laughing, and she didn't know what to do. No one she met was ever so open with their emotions. The first boy's line had seemed calculated to impress her, but now that she really looked at him, she could tell he was a bit nervous. She had no idea what was going on.

"Will you stop that?" the first boy said. "I am trying to make a good first impression."

"I think that ship has launched, Ned," the second boy said. "Possibly at light speed."

"Ned, is it?" Pendt said, trying to get control of the conversation. She didn't like facing this many unknowns. The *Harland* had probably launched by now, but she still didn't want to attract attention, and these boys were clearly magnets for it.

"Ned Brannick," he said. Pendt froze. "This is my brother, Fisher."

"You've scared her, Ned," Fisher said. "You didn't need to throw the Brannick at her already."

"I was being honest!" Ned said.

Everything was spiraling out of control. Pendt was going to get caught. She was going to be sent back. She was going—

"Let's try this again," Ned said. He held out his hand. "My name is Ned Brannick. I promise you, you do not have anything to be afraid of from me or from Fisher. We just want to talk. Can we go to a booth?"

Despite the noise and the crush of people, they were definitely starting to attract curious looks. And no wonder, two Brannicks talking to a total stranger. Pendt nodded and followed the boys to a booth in the back of the restaurant. A server appeared with menus, depositing one on the table for each of them.

"I'm starving," said Ned, who didn't look like he'd ever been on strict rations in his life. "We had two ore shipments come in today after literally months between deliveries. Can you imagine? Well, I mean, you were on one of them, so maybe you can."

Pendt didn't say anything. She didn't pretend to read the menu either. It would only list food that she couldn't afford.

"I saw you on the security camera," Fisher said. "Usually when a shipment comes in, one of us stays in the booth to monitor operations and the other goes down to help."

"What do you want from me?" Pendt asked. "Are you going to sell me back?"

"Sell?" Ned dropped his folksy pretense and sharpened to myriad edges at the word. "Stars, I was going to ask if you wanted us to *send* you back, but if you go straight to selling, maybe we should get right to it: over my dead body."

Pendt relaxed a little bit. These boys were strangers, but they didn't seem to be inherently cruel.

"I saw you," Fisher said. "You snuck off your ship, changed the way you were dressed, and made no attempt to return when you knew the timeline was tight. Furthermore, you probably know how your ship launches. It can't come back for at least a month, and that's if they burn *all* their fuel. You don't want to go back."

"No." Pendt was determined. "I won't go back."

The server came back and Ned ordered for the table. Pendt didn't understand any of the words he was saying, though she assumed they were all specific words for food. He didn't mention who was going to pay.

"So here's the thing," Ned said as he distributed the cutlery. "My parents are currently being held hostage by the Hegemony, do you know what that is?"

"It's what some people call the Stavengers," Pendt said. She picked at the serviette in front of her. It was, rather pointlessly, folded in the shape of a flower. She loved it. "Because it feels like less of an empire that way."

"We can argue about that later." Ned waved off her comment. "Anyway, since my father is gone, I am the Brannick, the only one on the station with the right genes to keep the station alive."

Usually at this juncture in the conversation there were awkward and ignorant questions about Fisher, but Pendt didn't so much as blink.

"I have to stay," Ned continued, "but I would very much prefer to go and fight in the rebellion."

"The rebellion?" Pendt said. "I'm sorry, we don't get a lot of current events on the *Harland*. I thought all that was more or less . . . finished."

"Not entirely," Fisher said quietly. "You're right about the empire not really having died, and neither did the rebellion against it. It's just more complicated now."

"And you want my help?" Pendt said. She pressed a hand to her chest. "I just found out there *was* a rebellion, I don't know anything about fighting in it."

"That's not what we want," Ned said.

"I saw you change your appearance," Fisher said. "It's not just a disguise; it's a full change. There hasn't been a gene-mage on Brannick Station with that kind of power for generations, and you can't be anywhere close to caloric maximum."

As if mentioning food had conjured it, the server returned with a heavy tray. When it was all on the table in front of her, Pendt started to hyperventilate. She'd never seen so much food at one time in her entire life.

"Hey, it's okay." Ned leaned over and awkwardly patted her on the shoulder. "I know rations are tight on a merchant ship, but we're a bit more relaxed here. Dinner's on us."

Pendt didn't move, even though it was becoming clear that the boys were not going to start eating until she did.

"You know exactly how many calories are on the table, don't you?" Fisher said. He took a small plate and broke a piece of something white in half. "This is bread," he told her. "You dip it in the oil like this."

It was the best thing Pendt had ever eaten. Tears sprang to her eyes, and for the first time in her life, she didn't blink them away. The *Harland* was gone. She was going to fucking eat.

"I'm almost afraid to tell you about cheese," Ned said, watching her closely. "And we're definitely going to have to ease you into sweets."

"Your ship wasn't just rationed tightly," Fisher said. "They starved you."

"They didn't," Pendt said around a mouthful. "They gave me enough to grow."

"But not enough to use the æther," Fisher said.

"Not safely, no," Pendt said. "I did it a couple of times as a kid before I learned how to suppress it."

"How angry is your captain going to be?" Ned asked. He broke off a chunk of bread and chewed it lazily. "I get the feeling that your ship kind of . . . sucked."

"She'll be furious," Pendt said. "But she can't justify the entire fuel supply to retrieve me. She has no way to recoup the loss. She might be back, but I don't think it'll be soon."

"What would have happened if you had stayed?" Fisher asked.

"My birthday is next week," Pendt said with a shrug. "Then I'd be old enough for a contract."

Ned swallowed and sat up straight. "Captain Arkady mentioned that they were on the way to meet up with a business contract," he said. "In a month."

"That was me, then, I guess," Pendt said. "Everyone on the

*Harland* has to earn oxygen, and for eighteen years, I've been almost entirely useless."

The boys exchanged a look.

"Fisher, I can't do this." Ned held up his hands. "Not now."

"Wait." Fisher leaned forward. "We might be able to work something out."

"'We'?" Pendt asked.

Ned took a deep breath, but it was Fisher who spoke.

"Even after your birthday, as a spacer, the head of your family controls where you work, right?" he asked. Pendt nodded. "So whenever your aunt comes back, you'll have no legal recourse to stay here."

"No," Pendt said. "My plan wasn't very thorough. I mostly intended to hide."

"This is going to sound like a lot," Fisher said. He pushed the vegetable platter towards her. She was fascinated by the colours. "But I think you should listen to my whole proposal before you react."

"See, you put it like that, and you're guaranteed to have a blow-up," Ned said. "We were going to offer to trade you all the credits you wanted and the nicest set of apartments on the station for a, uh, specific set of genes, but that won't be enough to save you if your aunt comes back."

"You want me to what?" Pendt said, horrified. It was everything she had left the *Harland* to avoid.

"It won't work anyway," Ned said. "So never mind."

"Listen to me, both of you," Fisher said. They stilled. "Pendt, it sounds like the *Harland* was awful and we want to help you escape from it if you can, but we're in a tight situation too. If anything happens to Ned, the whole station dies. You both want freedom from the roles you were born into, and you can secure it for each other."

"How?" Pendt asked.

"Marriage," Fisher said.

There was a moment of total silence.

"Of all the antiquated shit you dig up, you have to pick that?" Ned said. "It's unheard of."

"It's still legal," Pendt said. Her voice was speculative. "It removes me from my family and puts me in yours. My aunt can't claim me. You're the one who would make decisions."

"Actually, it's Fisher," Ned said, his voice flat. "He's older."

"You'd still need a baby," Pendt said. This was something she understood. This was a business arrangement. Just with higher-than-usual stakes.

Ned winced.

"Well, yes," Fisher said. "Specifically, one with a Y chromosome. Can you do that?"

Three hours ago, even thirty minutes ago, Pendt would have said no. But that was before bread. That was before cheese. That was before whatever "sweets" turned out to be.

"I've never done anything like that before," Pendt said. "Changing myself is easy, even with only a bit of extra food. It only took me twenty-eight grams of protein to do this to myself.

"But changing another person is more complicated. I can't imagine changing a grown-up. I've been around two developing embryos, though, and it did seem like I could have made the changes, especially if it were, uh, as personal and as early on as possible."

"You mean sex?" Ned said. Now he looked really uncomfortable.

"Can't we do it artificially?" Fisher asked. He winced. "Uh, for a given value of 'we.'"

"It's hard to explain," Pendt said.

"Humour me," Ned said.

"Well"—Pendt grinned at his discomfort—"when two people love each other very much—"

"Nope!" Ned held up a hand. "Just skip to the part after ejaculation."

"I can make sure a Y chromosome makes contact," Pendt said as delicately as possible to preserve his sensibilities. "It's easier than changing things afterwards, and it's easier when there are no medical distractions. Above all, it's easier when it's . . . inside."

"That doesn't make sense," Ned said.

"Where's Katla?" Pendt asked.

Ned pointed immediately and unerringly through the crowd.

"Oh," he said and downed the rest of his drink.

"So you get married, and your aunt can't control you," Fisher said. "And Ned gets a replacement Brannick. And the station gets stability."

"That's a very clinical way of putting it," Pendt said.

"I am trying very hard to not picture my brother having sex with a girl we just propositioned in a bar," Fisher told her. "It seems overly intrusive."

In spite of everything, or perhaps because her adrenaline was finally wearing off and her stomach was full for the first time in her life, Pendt burst into giggles. Her laughter was infectious, and Fisher soon found that he was joining in. Even Ned recovered from his indignity enough to smile about the situation. At least they all seemed friendly enough, since it appeared they were about to be legally stuck with one another.

"All right then, if it's okay with you?" she said to Ned. He nodded.

"We'll have to wait until your birthday for the marriage to be totally legal," Fisher reminded them. "If we do it before then, your aunt could contest it, and even though I trust most of the legal representatives on the station, it's possible she'd go somewhere else to argue it."

"Well," Pendt said. Ned blushed. "I guess we've got a week to get to know each other."

# 13.

THEY SPENT THE WEEK hammering out the details of the marriage contract—at Ned's insistence—and exploring every possible hypothetical way to create a viable embryo—at Fisher's. Since both of these things were in Pendt's best interest, and since they kept letting her eat whatever she wanted, they had her full cooperation.

"What if there are two contracts?" Pendt suggested on the fifth day.

Ned had been fiddling with the wording of the family association section of the contract for hours, trying to make it so that Pendt was entirely free of the Harlands while maintaining her freedom from the Brannicks.

"How would doubling the paperwork make anything better?" Ned asked.

"Well, the marriage contract is basically between me and Fisher, since he's the head of the family," Pendt said. "And what upsets you is the part where I belong to you as a result. So we write a second contract where you give that up, and we just . . . don't tell anybody. It'll be legal and it'll make you feel better."

Ned considered it.

"That works for me," he said finally. "I know I'm a decent human being and I would never take advantage of you, but the wording makes my skin crawl."

"Fisher?" Pendt asked. "What about you?"

"It doesn't bother me," Fisher said. "I'm not the one marrying you. I am glad you've got it settled, though, because I have more questions about, you know, the other part."

Pendt rolled her eyes. Boys were so squeamish. Now that she had full control over what was happening to her, she found that the idea of pregnancy and reproducing no longer bothered her. Since she had enough calories to access her connection to the æther, she had never felt more independent and alive. It was new and more than a little bit selfish, but she didn't care.

"I appreciate your consideration of my feelings and person," Pendt said. "But there are lives at stake. Everyone on the station, even if they don't know what we're up to, relies on us creating a viable genetic heir. If we were just experimenting, I'd be happy to give you all the eggs you wanted and work with them under controlled conditions in a medical laboratory, but we don't have that luxury. I need to be able to manage the variables myself, and this way, well, I can."

Fisher sighed. "As long as you're comfortable, I guess," he said. "I just . . . Bodies are important, you know? And you always thought you were going to lose control of yours, and I want to be *sure* that Ned and I don't treat you the same way."

Bodies were a fraught subject with Fisher. Pendt had told the boys the lurid details of her upbringing on the *Harland*, and their horror at her situation actually made it a bit easier to tell them the personal details. The only thing she hadn't talked about yet was Tanith's procedure. They were already tetchy enough about babies. Through all of it, Fisher had not volunteered any personal information, and Pendt hadn't asked. It was none of her business unless Fisher decided it was, and so far, he hadn't.

"You two could not be more different from my family," Pendt assured them both.

"Speaking of," Ned said. "There hasn't been anything in communications from the *Harland*. Is it possible they haven't missed you yet?"

Pendt considered it. The galley staff would have reported her absence immediately. It had been graveyard shift when she escaped, which bought her the most time, but either she'd have been missed at breakfast or Lodia would have noticed the vent as soon as she entered her quarters.

"They've definitely missed me," Pendt said. "They just don't have any way to come back for me, so there's not much point in talking about it. They can't threaten you over the comm channels, and they don't have any way to contact me directly."

"There's a benefit to that," Fisher said. "After your birthday, we won't have to keep you a secret anymore. You can have free run of the station and tell anyone you want who and what you are. You can even train with our gene-mages, if you like."

"That would be amazing," Pendt said.

A chime sounded softly, and Ned groaned. The boys still had to go to operations for their shift every day.

"It's only for a bit longer," Pendt said. "Then I'll be able to take your place, or at least help out."

When the boys were gone for work, the best part of Pendt's day began. She liked the Brannicks, and not just because they talked to her like she was a person, but when they left her alone, she was able to fully embrace what it meant to be a gene-mage.

She carried her breakfast tray to the calo-recycler. The boys had already put their trays through. Doing her own dishes on a full stomach wasn't so bad. Also, this model was much more advanced than the one on the *Harland*. All Pendt had to do was put the tray inside, close the door, and press a button. The whole galley in the boys' apartment was like that: clean, new, and easy to use. It was so different from what Pendt had grown up with that it didn't trigger any bad memories.

She snagged a few pieces of cheese out of the refrigeration unit on her way out of the room. Ned was correct: It was the best. Pendt had read about it the first morning after the boys left. It used to be made with the lactation products of large bovine animals, but early space travelers had learned how to make it without bringing the cow. Pendt appreciated their priorities.

Her favourite room in the boys' apartment was the greenhouse. It was a small enclosure off the lounge, sealed because of the high temperature and humidity. It was, Fisher told her, nothing compared with the station's hydroponics, which Pendt was welcome to visit as soon as it was safe to do so, but in the meantime, she was more than satisfied.

She chewed the cheese and swallowed it. It wasn't the best source of calories, but Pendt didn't care. She had options now, and her actual breakfast had been more than enough to give her enough fuel for the day. Anything else she ate was, at this point, entirely for her own use. And the greenhouse called to her.

It had only been a few days, but Pendt had learned more about the æther and her powers with it than she had in the entire time she'd been on the *Harland*. Ever since she was small and had been denied access to the ship's hydroponics, Pendt had wondered about plants. Now, with full access to them, she surrounded herself with greenery and just breathed it in.

Plants on a spaceship had two functions: They produced oxygen to supplement what the carbon scrubbers recycled, and they were a source of food. On Brannick Station, there was a third function, one that Pendt was coming to appreciate more and more every day she spent here. On the station, plants were also just *plants*. They were decorations or something to fiddle around with when a person was off shift. There were flowers that were pretty to look at and several herbs that provided no additional caloric value to food but did enhance its flavour. There were tiny trees that Fisher said his mother had tended and shaped, and something called a tomato, which Ned promised her would be ready in a few months.

In the greenhouse, Pendt was free to practice. She learned the genetic pattern of each plant and was quick to identify if any of them were in danger of getting sick. Most of the plants were clones, which made sense given the remote location of Brannick Station, and that meant that a weakness in one of them would quickly spread to the others. Pendt didn't find anything dire, but she was able to shore up the plants' defenses.

With the extra slices of cheese on hand, Pendt went deep into one of the little trees' genetic code. She knew from reading that trees were usually large, too large for a small apartment greenhouse. She wanted to see the part of the pattern that made the tree small. It took her a few minutes, but she saw it soon enough. It was like a switch had been flipped in the tree's childhood, making it small enough to stay in the Brannicks' home. It didn't cause the tree distress—if anything, constant babying had made the tree ludicrously healthy—but Pendt could see the spot where growth was stopped as clearly as she could see her own hand.

The difference with plants was that Pendt could change them after they had achieved maturity. She didn't just diagnose and shape; she altered, the æther flowing from her fingers as she worked it. With the calories to power her magic, it was almost easy, and she reveled in it.

"I wonder why I can change plants and not people?" she'd mused the second evening after giddily reporting to the boys what she'd learned how to do.

"Maybe there's a difference between being alive and being, well, *alive*," Fisher had theorized. "I don't think plants mind if you change them, but people are different. More complicated."

It was the best idea any of them had come up with, and it allowed Pendt to practice manipulating genetic code. This was the biggest change she had ever attempted. She'd made sure to ask permission—she knew the trees were special and she wasn't entirely sure what would happen—and both Brannicks understood why she needed to try.

Most of the plants in the greenhouse were young, newly grown in the past few months or perennials that reemerged every cycle. The little trees were old. Catrin Brannick had received them when she was a girl, and they'd been old then. It was the most complicated change Pendt had ever tried on purpose.

"I'm going to do my best," Pendt whispered to the tree.

Then she sank back into its code, found the switch that stopped it from growing. When she reached for it, there was no warning from her body that she was about to overextend or put herself in danger. There was only surety, a sense that this was what she was made for.

Pendt flipped the switch.

The tree didn't suddenly grow eight metres of new branches or anything. Externally, it was entirely undramatic. The leaves didn't even shake. But inside, Pendt could see the effects of what she'd unleashed. The tree flooded with light and water, making food for itself to support a growth spurt. It would still take time, since branches and trunk had to be reinforced to support each new inch, but the tree would grow, if she left it.

Pendt ate another slice of cheese and went back into the tree's pattern. She found the switch and flipped it back. The tree instantly went back to its former state, and Pendt checked for any lasting effects. As far as she could tell, there was no damage. The tree would probably grow a little bit, since it had expended the effort while Pendt was studying it, but aside from that, it was unchanged. Not only had she done the magic to alter the tree, she had correctly calculated how many calories she would require to put it *back*.

She pulled herself out of the tree and leaned against the wall of the greenhouse. It wasn't very comfortable, but she was tired. This too was a new feeling for her. She'd been exhausted before, pushed to the brink of system failure by a lack of calories, but this was different. This was the kind of tired that meant good things had been done, and that she would be able to do them again tomorrow. Her body was learning to rest normally, not because it was out of fuel.

Pendt ate the last piece of cheese and put the greenhouse to rights. She went back out into the lounge and curled up on the comfortable sofa. It was, she decided, more than fair that she get to take a nap before lunch.

# 14.

ON THE MORNING OF her eighteenth birthday, Pendt Harland slept in. It was the first time in her life she had ever done it. Usually, she was woken up by a chime calling her to work, or she woke out of habit. But this morning, she slept until her body was ready to wake up. Even then, she didn't get out of bed. She lay there, appreciating the fact that today she was a legal adult, and that she was going to steal herself from her family for good.

Eventually her stomach grumbled, something that made her laugh. It was no longer a desperate sound, something that spoke of emptiness and food withheld. Instead, it was an almost-pleasant rumble, a sound that remembered being full and would like to be again, thank you very much.

Pendt got up and pulled on her new clothes. Ned and Fisher had bought her five whole outfits and assorted sundries, something she found ridiculously excessive and they thought was the barest minimum. The idea of choosing what to wear was still strange to her, and she just grabbed whatever was closest, but she was start-ing to appreciate colour combinations and the feeling of certain fabrics against her skin. Today's outfit was a purple tunic that fell to her knees over yellow leggings and comfortable brown shoes. There was a yellow scarf in the closet too, and after a moment, Pendt took it out and tried to arrange it around her neck. She wasn't entirely pleased with the result, but she could look some-thing up later.

She'd left her hair long after escaping from the *Harland*, and watched a few vids on what to do with it. She lacked practice to do the fancier plaiting, but she could handle a ponytail high on the crown of her head. She liked the way the ends of her hair brushed against her neck like that, the soft touch of something that was hers.

Dressed and ready to face the day, Pendt activated the door to her room, and stepped out into the lounge. It was empty, but she could hear both boys in the galley. If they'd got up at the normal time, they would be finished breakfast by now, but Ned had men-tioned sleeping in too. They both had the day off from operations, barring an emergency that required Ned's genes.

"Good morning!" Ned said as she came into the galley. "You look nice."

Ned seemed determined to make this as weird as possible.

"Thank you," Pendt said.

She understood that he was trying to make them both com-fortable. In his world, people who did what they were about to do genuinely liked each other. From what Pendt had heard, Ned and Fisher's parents had actually been in love. It might be enough for

Pendt to have a thoroughly detailed contract, but Ned clearly expected himself to give her something else, and she tried to accept it as gracefully as possible. She did like both boys a great deal, even leaving aside the part where they helped rescue her and then came up with the plan to stay rescued. They were funny and nice, and different from each other in ways she was coming to appreciate. As for the rest, though, she wasn't really emotionally equipped to deal with it yet. And they seemed to understand that she would need time.

"Happy birthday," Fisher said.

"Thank you," Pendt said with a bit more enthusiasm. In the space of a week, her birthday had gone from a day to be feared to a day to be excited about, and she was pretty thrilled about it.

She sat down at the table and poured herself a glass of fruit juice. The boys both drank stimulants in the morning, but they made Pendt jittery. Fruit juice was on her long list of current favourite luxuries. Today's was a light pink.

"It's guava," Fisher said. "The crop ripened a few days ago. It's always all ready at the same time, and eventually all you can do is juice or freeze it."

"I like it," Pendt said.

"You like everything," Ned pointed out.

"I haven't tried everything yet," Pendt said. "We'll probably run into something I don't like eventually."

"Yes," Ned agreed philosophically, "and then you'll tell us that that calorie ratio is just *too efficient* to pass up and make yourself eat it anyway."

Pendt laughed. She was learning to be selfish, and Ned was

always ready to call her on it. He looked at her with a smile on his face, and Pendt felt a bubble of warmth in her stomach. It was nice to be liked.

They chatted amicably over breakfast, mostly explaining how operations ran when neither Brannick was present. Ned carried an alarm, in case a message was received that the Net was required, but aside from that, it was more or less the same. The schedule was light today. Most of the ships expected had arrived late last night, and nothing was supposed to show up until later in the evening. Still, sometimes there were unscheduled trips, and Ned had to be ready.

"Hopefully the universe has a sense of decorum," Ned said, "and we can at least get through the wedding without being interrupted."

The wedding they had planned was made up of two parts. First, there was the public handfasting. This was the traditional way two people joined their lives together, with no legal hold on the other. It had to be a mutual agreement, and either could leave at any time. Some people had arrangements involving property and offspring, but that wasn't a matter for public consumption. The second part, the marriage, would be done privately to ensure as few people as possible had access to the documents.

They finished their breakfast and Fisher took care of the dishes. He paused when he was done, and then went to the refrigeration unit.

"We made something for you," he said.

When he turned to face her, he was holding a circle of woven plants in his hand. Pendt recognized the flowers from the greenhouse. They were a riot of colours, but somehow the arrangement was pleasing to the eye.

"It's for your head," Ned explained.

Pendt took out her ponytail and used her fingers to comb her hair neatly down her back. She took the flower circle from Fisher and put it on her head. It smelled amazing.

"Thank you," she said. She had never felt this decorated. This intentionally impractical. With her hair down and the scent of the flowers wafting around her, she felt soft. And for the first time in her life, that didn't feel dangerous. "It's fantastic."

"The flowers have grown a lot since you got here," Fisher said. "We thought it was a nice way to show that you were already, you know, part of the family. Even without everything else."

Pendt smiled.

"Are you ready?" Ned asked. "People have already started to gather on the colonnade."

"I am," Pendt said. "Let's do this."

He offered her his arm and she took it. Together, they walked out of the apartment with Fisher behind.

The handfasting ceremony was short. Pendt hadn't met the person who did it, but they had a moment to chat before everything started.

"I'm a friend of Catrin Brannick, name of Dulcie Channing," the woman said. "I helped teach Fisher and Ned operations when they were little, and then after, well, after Ned and Catrin were gone. I guess I am sort of the foreman."

"It's nice to meet you," Pendt said. "I'm learning that family here means something different than it meant where I come from, and I'm glad that the boys had you when their parents were taken."

The crowd had grown quite large by then, and so Ned decided it was best to get things started.

Ned and Pendt held hands while Dulcie wrapped a long white ribbon around them. She spoke of commitment and cooperation, of work and play, of good times and poor ones. At the end of her speech, she asked both of them if they were ready.

"I am," Ned said.

"I am," Pendt repeated.

"Then before these witnesses, I declare you partners," Dulcie said. "May you bring one another peace."

Peace. Freedom. Fruit juice. Pendt couldn't help smiling up at Ned, and he smiled back at her. The onlookers cheered. They didn't know all the details, but they knew that the Brannick was working to secure their future, and they were pleased about it. Pendt looked at Fisher, who nodded at her. He wasn't the type to show emotions freely, but she knew that he was glad, and that he welcomed her.

The crowd dispersed as people came forward to shout congratulations at them, and finally, only a few stragglers were left. Ned thanked them and then pointedly led Pendt and Fisher into Dulcie's office, where they would take care of the marriage documents. Fisher quickly filled Dulcie in on what was going on, and the woman didn't seem entirely surprised.

"You messaged me saying your brother needed a wedding to a girl off a merchant ship," Dulcie pointed out. "I was aware that things might be a little bit . . . sensitive."

"You're okay with it?" Pendt asked.

"No," Dulcie said. "I am not okay with any of this. You're all too young. My friend is being held hostage. I know *very well* what Ned will do the moment there's a viable heir on the station. None of that is okay. But it's what we have to work with, and you're being smart enough to sort everything out as you go, so I can't really complain about it."

"I was kind of hoping you'd be happy for me," Ned said quietly.

"I am, darling boy," Dulcie said. She ruffled his hair. "I'm happy for you and I'm very proud of the way you're going about this. But that doesn't make it any less complicated.

"Now," she said, pulling up her screen, "let's finish sorting all of this out."

Dulcie had no additional suggestions for either of the contracts and commended them for thinking to include the second one. Everything was signed and sealed away in short order. The second contract was encrypted and stored in a separate file that only the four of them could access.

"So," Dulcie said wickedly when everything was sorted, "any big plans for the afternoon?"

"There are a couple of ships due." Ned's ears were pink. "But we're ready."

"I'm sure you are," Dulcie said.

She laughed as Ned all but dragged them out of her office. They went back the bar where they had met. It was quiet, since it was the dayshift, but the three of them sat at a table in the back and introduced Pendt to cake, since it was both her birthday and her wedding day.

Ned excused himself after a few hours to go take care of

operations, and Fisher and Pendt diligently finished all the slices that were left on the table before they went back up to the apartment.

"I am glad too, you know," Fisher said as Pendt took a seat in the lounge to wait for Ned. "What Dulcie said is right. It's not okay. But it's something, and it's ours, and that makes me happy."

"I understand completely," Pendt said. "This week has been amazing. I've never had so much time for myself—except when I was in the brig—and I don't feel isolated or weird. I've never really been happy, I don't think, and I'm not sure I'm happy now, but I am getting a good thing and I am giving a good thing, and that works for me."

They waited in comfortable silence until the door opened and Ned came in. He wasn't blushing anymore, and neither Fisher nor Pendt teased him. Instead, Fisher shook his hand and left, heading to operations for the darkshift. Pendt stood up. The scarf around her neck seemed very tight. Ned reached out and took the crown of flowers off her head. He set it on the table and held out his hand to her. It only shook a little bit.

Pendt took his hand, because it was hers to take, and squeezed gently. He smiled at her and drew her into his room.

# 15.

IT WAS A WEEK before Pendt was absolutely sure. Ned was diligent, Fisher was mostly absent, and neither of them asked her any questions. The first few times, Pendt was much more distracted than she had expected, but eventually she was able to focus. After that, it was fairly straightforward to sink into her own body and sort through the genetic patterns until she found two halves that would give the whole they were after.

"I'm not comfortable designing a person," Pendt told Ned one night between attempts. They were both naked and he touched her gently, as though to remind himself that she was real. "Not entirely, anyway. There's a difference between plants and people, like we talked about, and I don't like the idea of sifting through a person for what I want."

"I think I understand," Ned said. "No one would have designed Fisher, and he's perfect."

"My family wouldn't have designed me either," Pendt said.

"And if any of my older siblings or cousins had star-sense, none of the rest of us would exist."

So she didn't design the genes. She picked her own egg at random, releasing it into her uterus to wait. She made sure it connected to the right sperm, but her only requirement was that there be a Y chromosome. It was intention, she supposed, but not deliberate design. It was the most and the least that she could do. When she was sure implantation had been successful, she waited until Fisher was home for breakfast before telling them both at the same time.

"I'm pregnant," she said with no preamble, and then slathered strawberry jam onto her toast. Jam made bread even better than bread already was.

Ned froze with his own toast halfway to his mouth. Fisher waited a beat for him to say something first, and then pressed forward.

"That's good news," Fisher said. "Is everything in order?"

Bless Fisher for keeping everything professional. Ned ate his toast.

"Yes," Pendt said. "I would like to talk to the doctors here and get another opinion or two, and then we should work out a way to test if I can manage the station controls."

"That part's pretty straightforward," Fisher said.

"We aren't doing it that way," Ned protested, finding his voice at last.

"What way?" Pendt asked.

"When our mother was pregnant and our doctors confirmed I was male, they put her in a pod and sent her to Katla," Ned said.

"She kissed our father on the colonnade, and then walked into the docking bay all by herself. He took the lift up to operations and sent her through. The whole station stopped work, waiting for Katla to send her back. Either the Net would activate and catch me, or we would all be lost to space."

Pendt swallowed.

"Everyone was very relieved, obviously," Fisher said. He blinked several times to clear his eyes. "They love my mother, and they were glad of an heir."

"I would prefer a less dangerous method," she said. "But I understand if that is necessary."

"We'll take you to see Dr. Morunt," Fisher said.

Pendt started visibly. "Doctor who?" she demanded.

"Dr. Morunt," Ned said, confused. "He's the best one on the station. He's the one who took care of our mother when she was pregnant with us."

"The *Harland* doctor was named Morunt," Pendt said. "She was almost good to me."

"We can take you to one of the others, if you like," Fisher said.

Pendt considered it. Even if this new Morunt was related to the *Harland*'s, he had no way of communicating with her. He couldn't betray them, even accidentally. And it would be nice to see a familiar face, even if it was only familiar by proxy.

"No, it's fine," Pendt said. "Just let me get ready."

Brannick Station's Dr. Morunt was a heavyset man, well into his fifties. There was an infinitely higher number of body types on Brannick compared with the *Harland*, but Pendt still stared when she saw someone who looked different. She felt like an infant when she did it: Even working solely off genetic diversity, Brannick would have more phenotypes than the *Harland*, but she couldn't quite stop herself yet. She wasn't used to so many variations on living well.

He had the same open face as the *Harland* Morunt, but his was not weathered the way hers was, pale from years in space and gaunt from exact nutrition. He examined Pendt quickly and professionally, confirming that she was pregnant and that the foetus had a Y chromosome. He gave her advice on how to deal with her body as it changed and recommended a slight increase to her daily fitness regimen.

"Is it still a slight increase if I've never had a daily fitness regimen?" she asked.

He guffawed, which made her jump.

"Well, I suppose not," he said. "But walking around the station would be good for you, in any case. You're putting on weight very well, especially in your muscles, and I want to be sure your body learns to use them as they develop."

"Thank you," said Pendt. "I like how round I am starting to look."

"You are still distressingly scrawny," the doctor informed her bluntly. "If I hadn't heard through station scuttlebutt that you'd come off a merchant ship, I would be questioning your guardians about their mistreatment of you. As it is, I'm glad you're here now."

His vehemence was almost intimidating, but the fact that it was on her behalf made her comfortable. She asked the question that had been poking at her since Fisher told her his name.

"Dr. Morunt, I apologize if this is too personal, but do you have a sister?" she asked.

Dr. Morunt froze in the middle of putting away his stethoscope. His eyes grew sad and he had a faraway look on his face.

"I did," he said. "She's been gone a long time."

Pendt never pressed for information, and she didn't press now. It was clearly a painful subject, and she was holding enough painful secrets of her own to empathize completely.

"I'm sorry," she said. "Thank you so much for this examination. It has set me at ease."

"That's my job," Morunt said. "Next time bring the boys in with you. I haven't seen them in forever and they're going to need to know what's happening almost as much as you do."

"I will," Pendt promised. She slid off the table, the paper gown she'd worn during the visit rustling around her. Not being naked made a big difference when it came to medical exams.

Morunt nodded and left so that she could dress.


"There's one more thing I want to ask Dr. Morunt to do," Pendt said as they tucked into dinner that evening. Fisher maintained that nachos were a snack, not a meal, but Ned argued that anything could be a meal if you were determined about it. Pendt was inclined to agree with him: Somehow, melted cheese was *even better*. "If it doesn't work, it's easy enough to reverse, and it won't hurt either me or the foetus."

"What is it?" Ned asked.

"The Dr. Morunt on the *Harland* did the procedure on my mother, before I was born," Pendt said. "Sometimes Lodia would be implanted with two fertilized eggs, but only gestate one of them at a time."

"What happens to the other one?" Fisher asked.

"In the case of my brothers Willam and Antarren, it didn't work at all, and they were born as twins," Pendt said. "But Tyro and I were born a year and a half apart. I'm fine, so I know it works."

"But you're not carrying twins," Ned pointed out.

"No," Pendt said. "What I'd like to ask is that Dr. Morunt put the embryo I am carrying into stasis. That way, the chromosome will be present, I can still find out if the station will respond to me, and I won't have to . . ."

She trailed off, but Ned was already nodding emphatically.

"I didn't know that was possible, but if you can get it to work, I think it's a great idea," Ned said. "I know this isn't something you were worried about in terms of my involvement, but the idea of being a father scares the crap out of me and being an absent one is even worse."

"Your parents sound kind of awesome," Pendt said. "I think it makes sense that you'd be nervous about being a parent with that act to follow. All I have to do to surpass my mother is have a kid that calls me 'mother' instead of 'sir.'"

"What happens if you can't operate the station?" Fisher asked.

"Then I'll have Dr. Morunt reverse the stasis," Pendt said. "Once he walks me through it, I should be able to do it myself, actually. I only need his help because I want to be sure everything is as safe as possible for everyone who needs this foetus to be viable."

"I wonder if your mother had been a gene-mage, if she'd have been able to stop the twins from being born together," Ned mused. "Obviously, I am pro-twin, but I can understand how it might be a drain on resources on a spaceship."

"Everything is a drain on resources on a ship," Pendt said. "I'll make an appointment with Morunt for as soon as he's available."

Dr. Morunt was not entirely pleased with the idea but was mollified somewhat by Pendt's assurance that she had been fine as the "held-over" embryo. Pendt didn't ask any personal questions, but she had a feeling that the idea that his sister had helped her mother might have made him feel better about the procedure too. Or, at least it might if they were going to talk about it. Which they were not. Once they worked out the logistics, it took only a few moments.

Dr. Morunt placed his hands on Pendt's stomach, and Pendt followed him through her pattern as he worked, learning what he was doing as he did it. The embryo was still microscopic, only split a few times, and it was easy to contain.

*Later*, Pendt thought as they sealed it into the uterine wall, leaving it enough nutrients to sustain itself but not to develop. *Later I will be back, and you will grow.*

"Thank you, Doctor," Pendt said as Morunt withdrew his hands.

"I want the station to be safe as much as anyone else does," he said. "And you are a bit young to be starting a family, for all we desperately need Ned to do exactly that. He'll be leaving, I suppose? That boy was always restless, but since his parents were taken, it's even worse."

"The station will be safe," Pendt said. "I have promised to make sure of it. As for Ned, well, we both got something out of this arrangement, and both of us are convinced we got the better end of the deal."

"Come back whenever you like," Morunt said. "Working with you is like nothing I've ever done before. It feels like we could move the stars."

"I think the stars are best left where they are," Pendt said, a shudder running down her spine. "But I do want to learn the medical aspects of being a gene-mage, even though I think I like plants better."

"I'm happy to help," Morunt said.

Pendt left the office feeling lighter than she had felt since the morning after her wedding. She had no problem fulfilling her end of the bargain, and she would do it no matter what it took, but she was learning to factor herself into her calculations, and if she could make this easier on herself, she would. If it worked out, the station would be fine, and she would be able to give birth at a time of *her* choosing. Choosing was new for her, and she relished it. Getting one back at her family, who would have taken *all* her bodily choices away from her, was just a bonus.

She waved at a few shopkeepers as she crossed the colonnade. There were so many faces here, but she was starting to recognize them, and they definitely recognized her. The Brannick citizens didn't seek her out yet, not the way they did Ned when he walked the corridors, but that would come soon enough. She hoped. This was her home now, like the *Harland* had been. She had served the *Harland* because she had no choice. Brannick Station would have her, but they would have her because that was exactly what she wanted.

# 16.

TWO MORE WEEKS WENT by, and Pendt was healthy. She had been on Brannick Station for a month, and the changes in her body were amazing, even without taking the foetus into account. Her hair and nails were stronger, shinier. She walked around the whole station every day and it didn't cause terrible muscle cramps or leave her winded. She couldn't see the points of her bones sticking out of her skin anymore. She was softer. Rounder. Fuller. And every inch of her was better off.

She spent her days working in hydroponics, tending to the wide variety of plants there. Just that section of the station was as big as the whole *Harland*, and she loved every inch of it and all the greenery within. Even two weeks into her tenure there, the changes in the crops were marked. Everything was healthier, growing stronger. She caught rot before it spread and knew just by looking at a tree if the fruit was ripe. She had never been more pleased with her work.

Ned no longer invited her to his bed. After an entire life-
time of sleeping alone, she missed his reliable warmth, but she
wasn't about to push him. He organized his belongings, decid-
ing what he was going to take with him when he left, and sent
coded messages to his contacts in the rebellion, waiting to hear
his assignment.

Fisher showed her around operations. Ned could have done
it just as easily, but the whole point was to learn how to make it
work without him, so he stayed away. Pendt learned how each
part of the station worked, how they functioned as a whole, and
where the weak points were. She learned how to read schedules,
and what to do in myriad possibilities of emergency on the loading docks.

The embryonic stasis held. Dr. Morunt gave an official medical report that the foetus had stopped growing even though it was
still alive. Pendt could tell that for herself, just as she could tell
exactly how to reverse the procedure if she had to, but it was nice
to have a doctor to rely on again, and this Dr. Morunt was even
more considerate of her than the *Harland* one had been. All that
remained was to see if the foetus could, while in stasis, still operate
the station.

The first time Pendt tried to activate the Well, she passed out.
Ned stepped in and sent the ship on its way, and no one thought
anything was wrong, but Pendt was disappointed.

"We knew it might not work," Ned said later, in an effort to
make them both feel better.

"No, it did work," Pendt said. "Or, at least, it was going to. It's
a different kind of magic than I usually do. I never thought about

it, but your magic works differently than mine does. I went much too far into the station's operating system. I just need to practice."

Miraculously, the Well was scheduled for routine maintenance checks starting the next day. Everyone on the station was notified that it would be flickering on and off all day, and not to worry about it. Pendt fainted three more times and ate the equivalent of five days' protein ration, but eventually she had it down. She could turn on the Well on command.

"The æther's already there," she said. "I don't have to gather it together and look at it the way I usually would. I just have to input the key."

The Net was a bit harder to test, and since it was the one that could actually get people killed, it was imperative that Pendt get it right. If she could get it to work, then they would know it was safe for Ned to leave.

The system they worked out was a variation on the one they used to train Pendt on the Well. They made sure that there was a maintenance check on the schedule, and then Pendt practiced activating it with nothing to catch. When she could activate the Net on every try, they moved up to catching the uncrewed drones that arrived, empty, from Katla five times a week to be filled with any unprocessed oglasa that Brannick had accumulated. Pendt didn't miss any of them.

Finally, the day arrived when Pendt would catch a crewed ship. It was the *Cleland*. Choria knew what she was getting into, and trusted Pendt's record. Also, she was coming to Brannick to pick up Ned (and a few other rebel sundries she didn't tell them about), so it seemed fitting.

Pendt was very nervous.

"You'll be fine," Ned said. "Just pretend it's a drone."

"Choria doesn't even know you and she trusts you based on the work you've done," Fisher pointed out. "I can't think of a bigger vote of confidence."

Pendt thought she might throw up. She hadn't felt like this since she realized a month on Brannick passed, and there was no sign of her aunt. She was made of nerves, and all of them were on fire.

"Activating the Net," Pendt said.

She reached for the æther the way Ned did, the way the baby would someday. Usually she went into a pattern and felt her way to the parts that would welcome her changes, but this was far more direct. The switch was right at the top. Flipping it was easy. Anything beyond that, any change or alteration to the actual system, would drain her.

The Net surged to life and Pendt held it steady for five whole minutes as the *Cleland* landed in it. Pendt was new to hugs—activating was like throwing her arms as wide as a spaceship and catching the moving colossus—but if she thought of it as folding someone into an embrace, it was easier for her to execute.

"You did it!" Ned said. He picked her up and swung her around like she hadn't been putting on weight steadily since her arrival. She laughed, picturing herself as the ship and him as the Net, catching her.

Fisher grinned and clapped her on the back after Ned set her on her feet.

"We did it," Pendt said. "How long do you have?"

"Three hours," Ned said. "Choria wants me well on board before they leave. It's enough time for one more meal."

He grinned at her. She smiled back.

The three of them went up to the apartment one last time. Ned's things were mostly packed, but both Fisher and Pendt had independently got him gifts to take with him. Fisher went first.

"I know whatever you take has to be small," he said. "And that you might lose it in a storm of thrilling heroics, but I still thought this was a good idea."

He handed Ned a small package. Ned tore the paper off and smiled when he saw what he was holding in his hands.

After a moment, he handed the frame to Pendt so he could hug his brother.

Pendt looked at the image captured in it: two boys who were clearly younger versions of Fisher and Ned themselves, and two adults.

"Mum and Dad," Ned said. "Catrin and Ned the Elder. It's them I'm fighting for. I miss them so much."

"I miss them too," Fisher said. "And I miss you already, even though you're a jerk and you haven't even left yet."

"How am I a jerk?" Ned protested, laughing.

"You're supposed to be fighting for all of us," Fisher said. He was laughing too.

"I'll manage it somehow," Ned said.

"I have something as well," Pendt said. She had taken apart the crown that Ned and Fisher had given her for the wedding and figured out how to save the flowers under glass. The boys huddled over them. "I learned how to dry them and pressed a few into glass for you. It's very sentimental. I'm honestly kind of proud of myself."

Ned snickered and set the glass where they could all see it. The flowers were mostly red and orange, bright and warm against the cold and dark of deep space.

"I love them," he said. "No matter where I go in this wide, wide universe of ours, I will always think fondly of the top of your head."

"Fisher's right," Pendt said. "You are a jerk."

"Hey now, I was promised a last meal," Ned said. "Of course I'm a jerk. I haven't been fed."

"Back to the bar?" Pendt asked. "For old times' sake?"

There were several other restaurants on the colonnade that Pendt actually preferred, but once she started being sentimental, it became a habit.

"Actually, I was thinking more along the lines of several pieces of cake in place of a meal," Fisher said. He got up and went to the refrigeration unit. "And what do you know! No need to go out. There's a whole selection right here!"

Ned got plates and forks, and they divided up the spoils. Pendt noticed that all her favourite flavours were present, and that Fisher was sure to point out the ones she hadn't tried yet. She decided flan was disturbing. As the clock ticked down and they maxed out on the amount of sugar a human could consume, they ate more slowly, savouring each bite until it was time to go.

Fisher carried one of Ned's bags as they all went down to the bay where the *Cleland* was docked. People came out to see Ned off. Some of them looked frightened, but a medical release had been delivered to everyone on the station that morning, and they all knew that the Brannicks were still in residence. They reached the bay, and just the three of them were permitted inside. Pendt was glad to be free of the crush and grateful they would be able to say their goodbyes with fewer witnesses. She thought to duck away and give the brothers a few moments, but Ned pulled her close and didn't let her go when he caught Fisher in the other arm.

"I'm going to miss you both," he said. "I know this is ridiculous, but I feel like I'd be doing so much more if I was out there, fighting. I was never meant for the station, no matter what my stupid genes say, and we've always known it."

"I have," Fisher said. "I'm glad you found a way. I'm glad Pendt found us."

"You take care of my brother," Ned said, tears in his eyes. Pendt blinked. "He's always wanted to run Brannick Station, even though he's never said it. And he'll be better at it than I ever was."

"Ned, I—" Fisher started, but Ned held up his hand.

"We knew, Fisher," he said. "We've always known what our choices would be, if we had them. And now we do."

"Goodbye, Ned," Pendt said. "Come back to us."

"I'll bring fancy cheese," Ned said. "Maybe even an actual cow so you can make your own."

"I'm not cleaning up after a cow," Pendt said. "Not even for cheese."

"So ungrateful," Ned said. "I have no idea why I married you."

He pulled them both in tight for another hug, and then took his pack from Fisher. He carried two bags and a small weapons chest into the *Cleland*'s airlock, and waited while it cycled him in. Just before the door sealed, he turned around and waved.

Fisher and Pendt went up to the control room to wait for the *Cleland*'s departure. It took Choria about an hour to get everything settled once Ned was on board, and then the request to leave came through.

"It's all yours," Fisher said, gesturing to Pendt.

She stepped up to the controls and reached for the Well. It was almost second nature to her now, flipping the switch that would send the *Cleland* on its way. The Well flared to life, and the countdown started. Choria manoeuvred into position, and in a flash of rainbow, the *Cleland* was gone.

"We did it," Fisher said, slumping back in his chair. "We all got what we wanted. By some miracle we found one another, and we all got what we wanted."

He pulled her into a hug, squeezing her even more tightly than Ned had, and she could feel him smile against her hair. She looked up at him, answering him with her own grin.

"Let's go home," he said.

Pendt's smile grew even wider. Fisher had the station, Ned was free, and she was always going to be full.

# PART THREE

"SHAKE LIKE THE BOUGH OF
A WILLOW TREE"

S ome stories are so old that they take place on the ground, and this is one of them. Old stories are like oglasa, slippery and elusive, but there are plenty of them and plenty more, if you tend them properly. Stories keep forever, and they bring you life of a different sort.

Anyway.

There was a king. His kingdom wasn't very large, and there were other kings close by who were more powerful than he was, but generally speaking, he was doing okay. This was the time when kings were also farmers, expected to lead by example and tend their own lands. This king's lands were fertile, and he and his people tilled the soil and grew crops enough to see them through the winter.[1] It wasn't a particularly glorious experience, but it was a good one.

Tragedy came to the king's household. His family were taken from him—battle and sickness and old age—and then he was alone. He was stricken with an injury that made it very difficult for him to leave his tower. No longer could he follow the plough or thresh the grain. He couldn't bind the

---

1. See "seasons" in the datacore.

sheaves or carry the bales. He couldn't fix a fence or pick up a new lamb or drive the cattle into the barn.

All he could do was fish.

Fishing, as you know, is an industry to build an empire on, but that is the fishing of huge vessels and vast nets. Fishing can fail, of which you are also aware, when the shoals are scraped too thin. That is the collapse of empires, and a kingdom, especially a small one, is even more vulnerable to change. It is the work of hundreds of people, not one king on the bank of a quiet river.

At first, healers were brought in to make the king well again. They looked at his wound and applied their poultices and herbs, but none of them were successful. The wound did not worsen, but neither did it improve. The king struggled up and down the stairs, but still went every day to the river: It was the only way he knew of that he could help keep his people fed.

Then surgeons were brought in to make the king feel well again. They took his blood[2] and cleaned the edges of the wound with sharp blades or with hot metal. They bathed the wound with alcohol. The king bit into a leather belt to keep from screaming, but his wound did not improve. The castle grew dusty and damp since he couldn't fix the windows, but still every day he went to the river: There were hungry mouths in his kitchens and in his stables, and he had no way to give them grain.

At last, a priest was brought in to make the king feel well again.

---

2.  Don't ask.

"I don't know why I'm here," the priest said. "Unless you have particular feelings about your soul?"

"I think I'm good," said the king, "though if you have any other suggestions, I would appreciate them."

The priest thought about it for a few minutes.

"My lord," he said. "I will put out a holy writ, calling all the knights in the neighbouring lands to ride out in search of something that will help you. At least that will keep everyone busy."

"What will I offer as a reward?" the king asked. "My coffers are emptying quickly, and I have no family left to marry off."

"We will cross that bridge," said the priest, "when we get to it."

The years rolled on. The knights came and went, eyes shining with bright ideas and new hopes. Nothing worked, but several valuable trade agreements were agreed to and a new way of smelting iron was discovered in the process, so it wasn't entirely without result. Still the king lumbered from his bed to his spot on the riverbank, even when the fish stopped coming. His castle fell into disrepair and his people began to leave. He didn't stop them.

A young knight came one day with nothing. He hadn't been on a quest at all yet. He'd only heard that this was a good place to get inspiration. He sat by the king's side on the riverbank and listened to the stories of the days before, when the king had been able to plough and plant, and the lands had flourished.

"What if," said the young knight one afternoon, "I drove the plough?"

No one had ever offered that before. It had been years, but the king still remembered how to hitch up the oxen. He told the young knight how, leaning on a crutch the knight had made for him. It took forever, but they both enjoyed the work. The field wasn't large, but it would grow enough grain for the people who were left.

"What if," said the young knight a few days later, "your room was at the bottom of the tower, not the top?"

It had never occurred to the king that moving his room downstairs would help, but of course it did. Now that he no longer had to go up and down several times a day, he had more energy. His leg hurt less in the evenings and he slept better. He could walk far enough to reach the fishing hole, and not wait for smaller fish in the shallows.

"What if," said the young knight after a month had passed, "I stay, and you teach me everything you know?"

And the king had an heir and the heir had a quest and the little kingdom thrived.

Sometimes, it's a matter of asking the right question.

# 17.

A WEEK AFTER NED left, Fisher asked Pendt if she wanted to move out of the apartment. The question caught her completely off guard. She thought that things had been going well.

"I suppose I could," she said. "If there's a space for me to go. I don't need a lot. Am I allowed to take the possessions I've acquired with me?"

Fisher gaped at her.

"No, Pendt, that isn't the way I meant it," he said. "I would never send you off now that I've got what I need. That's terrible. And those things are yours. And even if they weren't, Ned left you an account. And—"

"I understand," Pendt said before he could get too hysterical. "I also understand that you might not like living with a relative stranger. I can go if you truly want to be alone."

This really wasn't going the way Fisher meant it to. He was trying to be nice. It was hard to be nice to Pendt. Not because she was difficult or surly, but because she was so bad at putting herself first.

"Look," he said. "Let me start over. Without taking my feelings into account, and without considering the well-being of the station: Do you want to live in your own apartment?"

It took Pendt a while to answer. She chewed thoughtfully on a piece of purple melon. He could almost see her weighing all the options and then trying *not* to weigh all the options.

"Do you want to live alone?" she finally answered with a question. "My only experience living by myself involved a closet with very poor air circulation. I knew that I'd have nicer accommodations here, but honestly, you are a good person to live with."

"I've never lived by myself," Fisher said. "This was my family's home, and then it was where Ned and I stayed. I hadn't thought about what being here by myself might be like."

There were already two areas of the apartment Fisher didn't go into. Pendt had never seen the suite his parents lived in, nor had she been through the doors of the office where his parents worked when they weren't in operations. Fisher did his work on the large table in the dining area, since the two of them ate in the galley. Now that she thought about it, Pendt didn't think Fisher had been into Ned's room since he left. If she moved out, he'd just haunt the lounge.

"Be selfish," she reminded him.

"I don't want to live by myself." He smiled at her.

"Neither do I," Pendt said.

"All right," Fisher said.

So they continued. Fisher slowly coaxed Pendt into leaving a

few of her belongings strewn around the lounge, and Pendt imple-
mented a cleaning schedule that Fisher was forced to admit did
make the apartment a nicer place to stay.

Work piled up for both of them. Though Pendt spent most
of her time in hydroponics, she had to be available at any moment to go to operations and turn on the Net or the Well. Every
time, there was a whisper of fear that she wouldn't be able to do
it, but every time, she did. Brannick Station lived. The air circu-
lated and the gravity worked and the lights pushed back the dark
of space.

Fisher's duties were increased now that Ned was gone, which
he had expected, and people came to him for all sorts of advice,
which he had not. He knew that Ned had often been approached
by station inhabitants—he'd stood to the side often enough while
it happened—but he wasn't prepared for the sheer number of people he now spoke with every day. It was exhausting.

Pendt noticed. He had dark circles around his eyes, and he
started drinking two cups of stimulant in the morning instead of
just one.

"I think you should teach me how to run the station," Pendt
said one evening. She was sitting at the table in the dining area
with a strawberry plant, trying to see if she could get it to flower
on command without ruining its internal workings. Fisher sat at
the other end of the table with several datapads and a star chart
spread out around him.

"What?" Fisher said. "I'm sorry, I was doing a calculation."

"I think you should teach me how to run the station," Pendt
repeated. "Or at least how to help you. My work in hydroponics

is mostly experimental, and I enjoy it, but I could spend half the time there and get just as much done. You need me."

"Are you sure?" Fisher asked. "You're already on call for operations at any moment."

"You're on call for the entire station," Pendt pointed out. "I don't know if you've noticed, but they've decided you're the Brannick now, and you are. Ned always had you to help him out, and your parents had each other."

"I hadn't thought of it like that," Fisher said. "But you're right. And it would be nice to have some help. But it doesn't have to be you. You're happy."

"I am," Pendt said. "But I live here, and someday I'll have this baby, and I want to know what we're all getting into."

Fisher considered it. It would be straightforward enough to get himself an assistant. Dulcie could help him find one, he was sure. But Pendt was already here, and he already liked her, and she was offering. It made a lot of sense.

"All right," he said. "Honestly, I think the station residents will be happy to see more of you. It's nice to know that there's a gene-mage overseeing your food, but they're used to seeing the Brannicks pretty frequently. They'll probably mob you once they realize you're accessible."

"I don't mind," Pendt said. "It'll take some getting used to. It's hard to explain. I've always had a job, Fisher. Since I was five years old, I was expected to earn every breath I took, and that was all it got me: oxygen and just enough calories to grow. It's nice to be—"

"Appreciated?" Fisher said.

"See, I didn't even know the word for that," Pendt said. She did of course, but she didn't mind when Fisher interrupted her. It was how she knew they understood each other.

"I'll teach you how to spell it," Fisher said, and Pendt laughed with him.

The next day, they entered operations together. Pendt drew a few speculative looks; everyone knew the schedule was clear until the afternoon, but no one said anything. She and Fisher went into the office that Fisher and Ned used to work out of, and she began to learn. By lunchtime, she was thoroughly overwhelmed and equally determined. By the end of the dayshift, she had more or less memorized the procedures for unloading ore ships, which wasn't a bad start.

Pendt became a regular feature in operations. The other operators soon started bringing questions to her if Fisher was busy. She couldn't always answer them, but her honesty and her willingness to learn made her very approachable, and everyone was charmed.

The colonnade was another place Pendt began to frequent. The food shops and restaurants were already familiar with her because of her work in hydroponics, but now she talked with all the shopkeepers and store owners. She learned the ins and outs of the gossip chain. Dr. Morunt often joined her for lunch, and the two of them would talk about æther, but never family. It was pleasant.

And the people loved her, which was the strangest thing. They would say hello in the morning when she walked past. A café owner would have a flavour of juice she hadn't tried yet and press it into her hand when she was on her way to operations. A parent would thank her for increasing the grain yield. A worker would wish her a good shift.

At first, she hardly knew how to react. She was thanked more times in a single morning's walk to work than she had been in her entire life. She'd never had this sort of power before—she'd barely had any power at all—and she found that she liked it. It wasn't like being the captain, where everyone relied on her whims and wishes. It was like being part of a crew, a real one . . . or a family. This was what it was supposed to be like. Mutual, genuine, caring, and real. She loved every single minute.

Her favourite time of the day was still the evening, when she and Fisher were home in the apartment, sitting in the lounge. She would read or watch him play a game, or they would talk about something she'd observed during the day. It wasn't exactly an idle time; Pendt often found her brain made connections during those quieter moments that had eluded her in the bustle of the day, but it was peaceful. With her feet up and a blanket wrapped around her shoulders, Pendt was comfortable. She liked comfort quite a lot.

Fisher sighed and put the game controller down.

"Are you tired?" Pendt asked. It was still early.

"No," he said. "This game is really better with two people."

Pendt had tried playing, but she didn't entirely grasp the difference between moving in real life and moving in the game and, as a result, just dragged Fisher down with her. He was patient, but it was hardly relaxing for either of them. He was used to playing with his brother.

"I know this is going to sound strange, but I think it must be kind of nice to miss your brother," she said. "I certainly don't miss any of mine."

"He's always talked about leaving," Fisher said. "And I always knew he'd find a way to. I even wanted it, because I knew I'd get to run the station if he left. But I didn't imagine this part. The part where he was just gone."

"I'm sure he feels the same way," Pendt said.

"Do you think we'll hear from him?" Fisher asked.

Pendt considered her answer. She had learned how station communications worked, but she knew that Fisher meant a more personal message. It was unlikely that Ned would be able to tell them anything detailed, but she suspected Fisher would appreciate literally anything his brother were to send.

"He might," she said. "When it's safe for him to do so."

They heard astonishingly little about the rebellion. It was nothing but rumours and stories, supplemented by the occasional ship that came out to Brannick Station for supplies. The bulk of the fighting was based out of the stations that were closer to the Hegemony's base in the Stavenger solar system. There wasn't much in the way of reliable news. Most of what they heard came thirdhand through merchants, who reported that prices on Katla were high, indicating an influx of people. They didn't know where Ned had been sent, and none of the news was specific enough for them to make even a general guess about where he was or what he was doing.

"What are you reading?" Fisher changed the subject.

"Just a story," Pendt said. "It's about a girl who finds out she's the descendant of a powerful warrior and has to find the others in her group to fight injustice."

"One of Ned's?" Fisher asked.

"Yes," Pendt said. "He told me I could use his library if I wanted. I don't touch anything else in the room."

"It's all right," Fisher said. "We both live here. Maybe I should start acting like it."

He looked at the mess of datapads and half-empty cups on the table in the dining area. He could use the office. Maybe leave the door open, but still.

"It would be nice to have that table available," Pendt said. "Not that I plan to have any parties, but it's the perfect size for the control group of the plants I'm experimenting on right now."

"I'd hate to get in the way of science," Fisher said. "Will you help me move tomorrow?"

"Of course," Pendt said. "But you have to wash the dishes."

"Done," Fisher said.

It was a new system, and they were still figuring it out, but they were going to make it work.

# 18.

THE BEST THING ABOUT Brannick Station, after being treated like a human being and having the availability of food, was time. The station clock ran the same number of hours as the *Harland* did, so there was literally no more time in the day, but Pendt felt every minute like it was new. She had places to be and she went to them, but there was none of the malaise that had dogged her in the galley or inertia that kept her from resting in the brig. Even her boredom was her own.

Not that Pendt was bored. She followed Dr. Morunt's advice and took to daily walks around the station. She learned the patterns of the ore processors and the dockhands. She watched the shop owners and food-service workers. They seemed happy enough, which was new for her, but she supposed that it might be because they were both paid a good wage and protected by a guild. While in no hurry to return to food service herself, Pendt could understand the joy in watching other people eat if you weren't hungry yourself. She liked cooking—Fisher told her that she was really "assembling," but she ignored him—and she was coming to understand the artistry of it.

Pendt imagined that the doctor intended her to stick to the colonnade and operations, but she ranged farther than that in an effort to get to know her new home. Parts of the *Harland* had been shut to her, and parts of Brannick were too, but they were mostly other families' apartments and private spaces. There was no public area that she was barred from.

So she walked. She covered every inch of the original station cylinder, the colonnade, and the docking ports. From that original construction, Brannick Station grew like two branches of a tree. One arm of the station housed her beloved hydroponics and other systems that kept the station livable, as well as all of the ore processing. Ships brought ore to Brannick from other places besides Alterra. The *Harland*'s run was the longest and slowest, and there were newer ships to make the other runs. Here, it was refined into solid burning fuel or smelted down for the raw materials that could make metal parts. The slag was dumped, which Pendt found absolutely enthralling. She was unaccustomed to waste.

After hydroponics, Pendt found herself drawn to the second arm of the station: the habitations.

The Brannick family lived in the "lowest" part of that branch, which is to say, closest to the colonnade and operations. Pendt was glad of this when she was summoned to the Net at all hours of the day, but she enjoyed exploring further. As the apartments got further from the colonnade, they got smaller, but there was no truly bad section to live in. It was merely assumed that those families with children would want to be closer to the schools and other amenities offered on the station proper.

Pendt loved the corridors the most. Families decorated their doors to differentiate their apartments from their neighbours'. Names and family sigils, along with flowers or legendary animals twined along the edges of each door, painted in bright colours. Some sections of the corridors were decorated completely to a single theme, and the themes changed depending on the days.

The corridors were divided by ladders and lifts for freight, and Pendt preferred to climb. It occurred to her on more than one occasion that the station's sense of direction was outdated. It would make much more sense if down was on the wall. But she appreciated the impracticality of it even more. Like a plant in her greenhouse, Brannick Station had grown and adapted, and its inhabitants had done the same.

There were small bowls outside the doors of many of the apartments. Pendt had seen similar setups in shops on the colonnade, and one of the techs in operations always had a water bowl underneath their desk. The inhabitants of Brannick Station kept the bargain of cats, offering water to the creatures who roamed the station and hunted vermin. They must feed them too, Pendt realized, since the environmental controls took care of most of the station's infestations. It was another sign that station life was different, and Pendt liked it. For the first time, being similar to a cat didn't bother her. She had a bargain too.

And then there was Fisher.

Pendt didn't spend all of her time thinking about him—that would be ridiculous—but when her thoughts drifted, more often than not, they landed on him. She had plenty to occupy her, between her plants and the Net and her changing physical form, but sometimes she had moments of quiet, and then she remembered him.

It wasn't like the way she thought about other people. Her family stirred up feelings of resentment and anger, and a sort of sadness she didn't enjoy. Thoughts of Ned made her worried and helpless. Thinking about the people she was meeting every day on Brannick Station made her feel welcome and at home, which she delighted in. But thinking about Fisher was something else.

First and foremost, there was the complication of being married to his brother. She and Ned had an understanding, of course, and Fisher was very well aware of it, but even leaving the legality of everything aside, Pendt knew that a wedding meant something to the Brannick boys that it didn't mean to her. She wanted to respect that as much as possible, but sometimes the light fell on Fisher's hair, or she caught the line of his shoulders and . . . well, she hardly knew what to call it.

Pendt knew that Fisher cared about her. Respected her. Valued her. All three of those things were new—except for value, but even that was different from the way Arkady had valued her—and Pendt was adjusting to them. She didn't want to read anything into his treatment of her, just because he was being nice. Yet the pages of the books that Ned left behind guided her mind down new and exhilarating paths, and she worried that she was starting to develop an imagination in spite of her best efforts.

The easiest thing would have been to talk to Fisher, of course, but Pendt wasn't quite there yet. She liked having her mind to herself. She liked the way her thoughts spilled over themselves, concocting increasingly unlikely scenario after increasingly unlikely scenario. She'd never had this sort of time to herself before, and she was hesitant to share it before she had finished wallowing in it.

So she didn't. She spoke to Fisher all the time, of course. It was impossible not to. They lived together and worked together, and Pendt tried not to read between the lines of his everyday conversation. But he was good to her. And he didn't have to be. And she didn't know if that meant anything.

And it was driving her insane.

After a few days of thinking about it (and nearly ruining half an acre of sunflowers through inattention), Pendt arrived at the only conclusion she could. She was a spacer, new to staying in one place. She was still adjusting. Fisher knew that. They were getting used to each other, both at home and in terms of running the station. Fisher was learning how to live without the constant support of his family. Pendt was learning how to live without the constant fear of hers. They had a lot of things to get through, and even if Pendt had a rough idea of where she was hoping they would end up, she had to wait until Fisher was ready. She was the station, this time, and he was the long-haul ship. He'd arrive when he arrived, and she could guide him into port.

More than that, she understood that he might be slow to decide. His whole life had rerouted, and even though he was getting most of what he wanted, it was still an adjustment. And it was a permanent arrangement. They had to live with each other at least until Pendt gave birth, which she was in no hurry to do. If he was going to be cautious about how he treated her, she could respect that. There was nowhere else either of them wanted to go.

In the meantime, Pendt had a friend. Ned was her friend as well, of course, but he was gone. Dulcie was more of a mentor, and the other people Pendt had met on the station were too new for her to trust completely yet. Fisher was different. He had welcomed her and plotted with her and helped her steal herself from the *Harland*. That was friendship, and Pendt was happy for it, even if there were times at night when she rolled over and was sad to remember that she was alone. She did everything she could to make Fisher's life as easy as he was making hers, from learning his favourite foods to practicing that stupid video game until she was kind of passable at it.

She'd served her family and her ship for her entire life, and it had never felt like this. This was reciprocation. This was joy. This was good work well done and effort appreciated. Pendt learned to receive as well as give and found that each of them was made better by the other. And at the centre of everything was Fisher. As her world got bigger and more complicated, he stayed unmovable and solid. And she wanted nothing more than to make sure they had each other forever.

It was the bargain of cats, and she was patient. All she had to do was wait for Fisher to put out the bowl.

# 19.

**"WHAT'S IT LIKE, USING** the Net?" Fisher asked.

Pendt considered her answer. She set her book down on the sofa and turned to face Fisher, who was sitting at the other end. She crossed her legs underneath her and leaned against the cushions along the back for support. Softness was still something she was getting used to, and the sofa cushions were particularly nice. Fisher set his datapad down and mirrored the way she sat.

"It's different from using the æther on my own," she said. "I don't change anything or make anything grow. The magic is already there, locked in place. It's strange because I have to go through the foetus, but once I do that, it's like I have a key."

"All Ned had to do was press a button," Fisher said. "But I suppose that's what happens when you *are* the key."

"Yes," Pendt said. "It's cruel, either way. To put so much life on a single person's chromosomes. Space is harsh and the *Harland* was far from pleasant, but at least my aunt never lied about the fact that all of us were needed."

"It's control," Fisher said. "The Stavengers were dying, and they wanted to make sure we couldn't flourish without them. I think that's what made Ned so angry. He never shirked his duty, but he felt like any problem Brannick Station had was his fault. He was desperate to fight, personally."

"You never were?" Pendt asked. Fisher had never mentioned wanting to accompany his brother, even just to know what he was up to without waiting for dispatches.

"No," Fisher said. "Don't get me wrong, I want the Hegemony's hold on the stations gone, but my style of fighting is different."

"Rebellion is a new concept to me," Pendt admitted. "I'm not sure I understand what you mean."

"Well, someone has to make sure the fighters eat," Fisher said. "And someone has to make sure that ships get sent where they need to be, and that ore is processed for new weapons."

"Someone has to run the hospital," Pendt said. "And make sure they have a place to rest when there's a break in the fighting."

"Exactly," Fisher said. "There aren't usually stories about those people, but they're just as necessary. Ned understood that. He appreciated what I wanted to do. My rebellion is that I love myself and I want to run this station anyway. I want to be the Brannick."

For the first time since she'd known him, Pendt wanted to ask. She shifted in her seat, moving closer to him without meaning to. It was always comfortable, being close to Fisher. That didn't give her the right to pry.

"Everyone gets that look with me, eventually," Fisher said.

"But it's been weeks, and you have never asked. Not once. You've never made me feel uncomfortable and you've never judged me, and you've never said a word."

"I have a slight advantage," Pendt admitted.

He smiled, and she relaxed. She put her head against the cushions, very close to where his hand was resting.

"No one ever said it, but I've always known I'd be more useful for the Brannicks if I was a girl," Fisher said. "I could have made an alliance with another station, traveled and made connections for trade. Ned could never have done that. His work always had to be here."

"But you're not a girl," Pendt said. "And you never have been."

"No," Fisher said.

"My family told me I was useless all the time," Pendt said. "I was a waste of calories until I was old enough for them to use. My rebellion is that I left them before I could pay them back."

"You don't owe them anything." Fisher took her hand in both of his and squeezed it. "A person is worth more than what they're born as."

Pendt looked at him.

"Right," he said. "I guess I expected you to challenge me, somehow. To make me justify it. My parents never did, and Ned certainly didn't. But sometimes a new person comes to the station, and I can just feel it wafting off them."

"That's a disgusting image," Pendt said, wrinkling her nose. She thought for a moment, her hand still warm in Fisher's, and then spoke again. "I'm not saying that what we've gone through is the same. It actually couldn't be more different. But I think perhaps my upbringing made me sympathetic to yours, if that makes any sense. It's not the same, but it's similar enough that we understand each other."

"I think you understand me more than I understand you," Fisher said. "Just thinking about your family makes my blood boil."

Pendt smiled at him. She didn't really need it, but it was nice to have someone who was always ready to ride to her defense. She turned slightly and rested her head against his shoulder instead of the sofa. It was definitely not as soft, but somehow it was even more natural.

She'd become quite familiar with Ned's body before he left, and he with hers, but there had never been this sort of comfort between them. There was always a task. Perhaps more on her part than Ned's. He had never pushed her, but now that she had read a few books and eavesdropped on a few dinner dates at the bar, she was aware that he had been less concerned with the end goal than she was.

Pendt had never learned how to be quiet with Ned. On the *Harland*, all relationships were transactions, and that was how she'd interacted with him. He'd been good to her, much better than anyone else had ever been, but she still thought of it as part of their bargain, the way in which she purchased her freedom from her family. She wasn't entirely sure she wanted the sort of relationship with Ned that she had with Fisher. Ned was brash and charming, and she liked him, but Fisher was steady and sweet, and she liked that much more.

Fisher had gone still when she put her head on his shoulder. She looked up at him to make sure that he was comfortable. She didn't want to make him uneasy. His eyes were closed, and he was breathing slowly, like he wanted to remember what this felt like before he let himself believe that it was real enough to see. He was still holding her hand, but he shifted so that their fingers were linked.

"Do you love Ned?" Fisher asked. His voice was low, like he was afraid of the answer.

"I've never loved anyone," Pendt said. "Not like you mean, anyway. I like him, obviously. He's almost impossible to not like. But no, I don't love him."

"I do," Fisher said.

"I know," Pendt said. "I wish I did, if that makes sense. I wish I loved my brothers, and I wish I knew who my father was, and I wish my mother was more like yours. I never wished any of that before I got here. You made my heart grow, and now I have to figure out where everyone fits inside it."

"Even me?" Fisher asked. This time he looked at her. He was very close.

"Especially you," Pendt said.

Ned had never really kissed her. There had been mouths on skin and on other things, but never the warm press of his lips on hers, the soft searching of his tongue.

Fisher kissed her slowly, like he wasn't sure he was allowed. He leaned down for an eternity before he touched her, and she thanked her lucky stars that she hadn't skipped the steamy parts in the books Ned had left so that she knew to turn her face to his and wait. After that part, though, the books proved completely useless.

Fisher's hands slid up her arms, drawing her body close to his.

It was a precarious balancing act, but she trusted him to bear her weight. He held her face gently in his hands, like she was precious and good, and his mouth moved over hers. She was warm, suddenly, right down to her toes, and surged towards him. The shift in weight pushed him back against the arm of the sofa and pressed her chest against his. He laughed, breathless, and caught her in his arms, straightening his legs beneath her so that he could hold her body more comfortably. He kissed her again.

Her only point of reference for the feelings he was stirring in her was Ned, and she really didn't want to think about Ned right now. Pendt didn't know what to do, but Fisher didn't seem to care. He had to know that her only experience with this type of thing was with his brother, but nothing they had ever done was this intense, this personal. She pulled back a bit from his mouth, and he didn't stop her. He looked at her, unblinking. There was no regret in his gaze.

Pendt blushed, turning bright pink as he stared at her. It was ridiculous and she couldn't do anything to stop it. She buried her face in his shoulder, unable to take the frankness in his eyes any longer. She started to giggle and couldn't stop herself. Fisher laughed and tightened his arms around her. It felt like home.

"I'm glad you're here," Fisher said. "It's complicated and kind of a mess, and I have no idea what the future is going to bring, but I'm glad you're here."

Pendt knew that he meant the sofa specifically, not the station in general. She was glad too, though she didn't trust her voice enough to say it. Fisher didn't seem to expect an answer anyway, which was another reason she liked him, if she was honest with herself. He understood her before she spoke, and he understood her when she couldn't.

They sat in silence for a time. Pendt wondered if this was the first time in her life she had ever been so at ease, so content. It was an ugly question but confronting the wretchedness of her child-hood helped her move further away from it. She decided that it didn't really matter. She had Fisher and Fisher had her, and they were going to see what came of it.

She'd dozed off by the time Fisher's communications unit chimed, indicating that he had a message. If it had been her unit, she would have bounced up immediately: that always meant they needed her for the Net or the Well. Fisher's communications were important, but rarely quite so urgent, and she watched him as he slowly reached out with one long arm to snag the datapad off the table.

He sat up so abruptly that she was nearly dislodged onto the floor. Both of his hands were on the datapad, so she didn't have anything to hold on to. She scrambled to keep her balance and stay sitting on the sofa, and by the time she'd sorted herself out, Fisher's face was as pale as if all the blood in it had drained out.

"What is it?" she asked.

But she knew. She couldn't have said how, could not have given a logical explanation, but she knew.

Fisher handed her the datapad, and she read the words she hadn't allowed herself to consider long enough to fear. The *Cleland* had been captured and destroyed in battle, with all hands aboard.

Ned Brannick, the bright boy who did his best to save her and save everyone else, was dead.

# PART FOUR

"YOU MAKE A FOOL OF DEATH
WITH YOUR BEAUTY"

S ylvie Morunt was a daughter born to a man who wanted only sons. She gave up trying to understand her father when she was quite young. Some people are bigoted, and you cannot reason with them. They have no redeeming qualities, even if they are talented in other arenas. It was not Sylvie's job to rehabilitate him.

She became a doctor because her brothers did, and she loved them. They were all gene-mages of varying ability, and Sylvie tagged along to their classes on Katla Station until the teachers accepted her presence. She was young, but she was proficient, and good at working hard, and soon enough she and her brothers were graduating. She was seventeen, which will be important in a minute.

Katla Station flourished. It mostly stayed out of the rebellion, though it did provide raw materials if the rebels were buying. Those who ruled there considered themselves free enough already and weren't in a huge hurry to help other people if it didn't directly benefit them. The people mostly followed suit because it was safe. Those few who did feel the call to fight left and were rarely heard from again.

The Morunt family had no rebellious tendencies. The father was heavily involved in business and was not the sort of person to care who he traded with so long as the money was good. He haunted docks for new opportunities, and that is why he was ready when the *Harland* came into port.

The *Harland* didn't come to Katla very often. Passage through the Well at Brannick Station was outside their operating budget, but they had a delivery to make, and so the captain had decided it would be worth the expenditures. None left the ship but him, and the cargo. The first was normal for a spacer family, but the cargo manifest was a little too perfectly accounted for, and the Morunt patriarch sensed an opportunity.

Sylvie often wondered, in the years that followed, what would have been different if she hadn't stayed home that day. The *Harland* ran on a tight schedule, and if her father hadn't been able to find her, they wouldn't have stuck around to wait. But she was home with her middle brother, waiting to hear about a job he had applied for. She was too young to work officially yet. She had to wait until her birthday so that she could sign a contract.

Her father didn't give her time to pack. There was no room for nonessentials in space, he told her. The Harlands would give her anything she needed. It all happened so fast that she didn't realize what was going on until he'd dragged her all the way to the docking port, her brother rushing behind them, yelling questions that went unanswered.

The captain of the *Harland* looked her over and nodded. Her father let go of her arm, and Sylvie tried to run. She didn't know where she was going to go, but some instinct told her to try. They caught her immediately, of course, and the captain dragged her screaming through the airlock.

Sylvie learned very quickly that no one cared if you screamed in space.

She was taken to the infirmary and given a daily allotment of calories. She tended to the Family. There were two girls who were a few years younger than she was, but in *Harland* years, they were almost adults themselves and ready to take their places on the ship, but they ignored her. She thought she had been lonely on Katla, when it was just her brothers and the older students, but now she had nothing, and no one person in the universe cared about her.

The *Harland* returned to Brannick Station and began another circuit of the mining complexes. Back on Katla, each Morunt brother left. In getting rid of his daughter, the father had also lost his sons. He turned lonely and bitter, blaming her for everything that he had done. The boys scattered to different stations, knowing that they would probably never see their sister again.

Sylvie got older. There was no chance of her leaving the ship. The places they stopped were all dangerous, and by the time she returned to Brannick Station, two decades had passed. The *Harland* had a new captain, and several children had been born. Sylvie had seen them all from conception to their first breaths, but there was nothing else to their relationships. She kept them healthy and they let her eat.

Two years into her second circuit with the *Harland*, a new

child was born. Sylvie knew immediately that the child had magic like hers, that someday she would use the æther to manipulate bodies. She'd also learned enough about the people she served to know that they would not be welcoming of such a child, worse than her father had been for her. They would actively shunt her aside until they could use her, and she would grow knowing what kindness was only by its absence.

It wasn't Sylvie's job to tell what kind of magic her patients had, so she didn't. She watched the girl get older, watched as she was forced to betray herself at five years old and was then pushed aside. She couldn't do anything to help, and so Sylvie mostly ignored her.

But then she remembered that her brothers had loved her. That her teachers had encouraged her. That even the most senior students had congratulated her if she got a higher mark than they did. No one deserved misery. Sylvie couldn't do anything big, but she might be able to help the girl in small ways. There was no reason to revisit the cruelty done to her onto someone else, just because she could.

So she watched, and she waited. She helped regrow a fingernail and taught the girl to control her power. She pretended not to notice when the girl slipped past the limits of the medical texts on board and started reading legal treatises and stellar cartographies. And when the time came, she gave the girl enough warning to hoard calories and escape.

Sylvie Morunt had come to the *Harland* with nothing, and she'd never leave it. But they'd never get her soul.

# 20.

NED BRANNICK'S FUNERAL WAS uncomfortably similar to his wedding, and all the more so because the two events took place so close together. Dulcie Channing officiated, and Pendt and Fisher stood at the front of the assembled crowd. The colonnade was crammed full, with people on the balconies to watch and screens in all the places where work couldn't stop, even for this. The main difference was that everyone was sombre and quiet this time. And, of course, that Ned himself wasn't there.

The colonnade had been decorated with black banners to commemorate his loss, and only a skeleton staff was working in operations so that as many station residents as possible could attend the service in person. They wore their normal clothes, but tied black ribbons around their arms, or wove them into their hair. There were flowers everywhere, by Pendt's request. Ned had given her flowers when he showed her to the greenhouse that first time, and it was how she wanted to remember him. The funeral was a bit more colourful than it might have been otherwise, but no one took offense. They all knew what flowers were to Pendt. With no body to look at, the event was a bit shorter than it might have been, but Pendt still felt every moment of it weighing down on her shoulders.

When Ned was alive, out there in the black void being heroic, people had accepted Fisher's rule and Pendt's assurances. Without the promise of his return, they might need her to give birth as soon as possible, to ensure the baby was safe. Without the promise of his return, Fisher might not be enough for them, and that would hurt him more than anything. Pendt couldn't stand the thought of Fisher being hurt any more than he already was, not if she could help it. She vowed to do everything she could.

Dulcie was winding down, and turning to offer Fisher his turn to speak, but Fisher had frozen where he stood. It was easy for Pendt to imagine what he felt at the loss of his brother. Pendt just took what she felt for it and multiplied it by several fingernails. Unwilling to let the moment pass without a speech from someone in Ned's family, Pendt took a few steps forward. No one shouted her down, so she went all the way up to the podium Dulcie stood at and turned to face the crowd.

There were so many of them. She'd spoken at her wedding, repeating Dulcie's phrases, but her back had been to the crowd, then. Now she faced them all, and she could see their worries and their fears. She'd never spoken to this many people at once, not even close, but she had to. She took a deep breath. This was for Ned. This was for Fisher. She could do it for Fisher.

"Ned Brannick was one of a kind," she said. "Which is something of an accomplishment for a twin, from what I gather."

Fisher smiled at that, and a polite chuckle rolled through those who were assembled. They loved the boys, she realized, they didn't just serve the Brannicks because they had to. They were loyal, the result of generations of mutual goodwill.

"I didn't know him very long," Pendt continued. "But I know that he was the sort of man who tried to save one person while remembering to do his duty to everyone who relied on him. I know that, because that's why I am here."

Brannick Station knew the rules. They knew what was required to keep the station running. They knew Pendt was pregnant, and that she was sustaining the pregnancy. None of them seemed to hold it against her, now that she was standing in front of them. She was doing the job she had been brought on board to do, but it was time to tell them how much she was committed to serving the station.

"Many of you were at my handfasting a few weeks ago," she said, an unexpected catch in her voice. "You know that I promised Ned to help him and to make sure his line continued. You know that I've been trying my best to learn how to run Brannick Station."

They were nodding, now, and murmuring to one another. Yes, they had seen her working in hydroponics. Yes, they knew what she was trying to do in operations so that Fisher could have a break sometimes.

"We didn't plan to tell you, but the day that Ned and I were handfasted, we had a second ceremony. A marriage."

Gasps of surprise rushed through the crowd, echoing Ned's protests from that day so few weeks ago. Marriage was beyond serious. It meant Pendt was *theirs*. It meant Fisher could order her to do whatever he liked, even if she knew he never would. It meant that, for Pendt, there was nothing beyond Brannick Station anymore.

"I'm telling you now, because I want you to know how committed I am to you," Pendt said. Her voice rang out above the colonnade. "I was born a Harland, and raised a Harland, but I became a Brannick. I did it a little bit for me, I won't deceive you. I wanted a home that I could never be taken away from. But I knew that I was also agreeing to a covenant with you, Ned's people, not just with him."

They pressed forward, hands reaching out to touch her. Dulcie put a hand on her shoulder to keep her steady. Fisher looked a bit alarmed but covered it well. He came to stand beside her.

"We know that it is a time to mourn," Pendt said. "We know that Brannick Station has mourned more than its fair share in recent years. We know that you need time to grieve and time to understand how the changes will affect you.

"But we want you to be sure." She looked down, and then back at the crowd. "I want you to be sure: I will do my best for you, always. This is my home, and I can't begin to explain to you how important that is to me. I am yours for as long as you need me, Brannick Station."

Fisher took her hand as the crowd threatened to overwhelm them. No one was angry, they just wanted to be close to her. She thought they would try to touch her belly, where the next Brannick hibernated, but they didn't. They pressed their hands against her shoulders or the top of her head and called her precious and good. Many of them were crying, and Pendt was powerless to stop her own tears. A sure sign she was a Brannick, she thought. No more taking it on the chin. Brannicks fought back.

It took nearly an hour to extricate themselves from the crowd. Fisher never relinquished her hand the entire time. It was the most he had touched her since the night they learned of Ned's death. Fate was especially cruel to tie those two moments together, Pendt thought. She didn't know if Fisher was ever going to let her replace that memory with something else. She didn't know if she wanted to. It was so strange, to think about kissing one Brannick boy while news of the other's death streaked its way across the stars to where they sat.

That sort of thinking could drive a person spare, Pendt realized. She knew guilt ate at Fisher, and he wasn't ready to pull himself out of it. Pendt was more rational than he was, at least when it came to this. She refused to let herself be drawn into the pointless sea of what-ifs. It wasn't very much fun. She wanted, more than anything, to lose herself to feeling. But Fisher needed her. Brannick Station needed her. And she had promised.

Pendt led Fisher back up to their apartment and settled him on the sofa in the lounge. She knew he'd been drinking stimulants since the news came, trying to stay awake to make arrangements and do his normal job in operations, so she brewed him a tea instead. It had no stimulating effects, as far as she could tell, but it tasted nice and it was warm to hold, and maybe that would help.

"Ned never questioned who I was, you know," Fisher said

when Pendt handed him the cup and sat down with her own. "He said he'd watched me grow, and he knew better than anyone. Which is ridiculous, and was even more ridiculous when we were five, but it still helped me a lot when things were challenging."

"Ned had a way with people," Pendt said. "I don't exactly trust easily, and his opening line was terrible."

"Right? I thought we'd lost you for sure," Fisher agreed. He took a sip of the tea, which Pendt counted as a win. She knew exactly how many calories he'd eaten in the past few days, and it wasn't enough. The tea didn't have much to offer, but perhaps it would remind him to put things in his mouth.

"I think we could have resented each other, you know?" Fisher said. "I wanted what he had, and he wanted what I could do, and neither of us was content with what life gave us to start with. But instead he made us a team, and we did everything together."

Fisher's voice caught in his throat, and Pendt braced herself. Fisher hadn't shown much emotion to her since they'd got the news, and she didn't mind. Fisher needed to grieve in his own way. But if he was going to fall now, she was going to do her best to catch him.

"I knew he'd leave," Fisher said. "I always knew he'd leave as soon as he could. And I thought about being alone, but I didn't think about being alone forever. I thought he'd come back. We were always a team. But no one comes back. Brannicks go into space and the Hegemony takes them, one way or another."

There was an edge to his voice she'd never heard before. He was angry, beyond furious, and she couldn't help him.

"Will you go to avenge them?" she asked delicately. "No one would blame you if you wanted to join the rebellion now."

"I can't leave you here alone," Fisher said.

"Yes," Pendt said. "You can."

It hung there for a moment between them.

"I *won't* leave you alone," Fisher said, his promise low and harsh. "The Hegemony has taken my whole family, and I want to hurt them, but we will do it from here, you and I. We will find a way."

"I'm glad to hear that," Pendt said. "We still need a true Brannick."

"After today, they'll all think you're the truest Brannick in a generation," Fisher said.

He set his cup down, and Pendt noticed that his hands were shaking. She set her own cup down and reached out to take his hand in hers. He looked at her, wild grief in his eyes as the tears started to fall.

"I miss him so much." Fisher's voice was hoarse with tears. "I've never been without him and I don't know what to do."

"We'll find a way," Pendt promised. "I don't know how, but we'll find a way."

Fisher hiccoughed as the tears started to fall freely. He pitched forward and landed with his head in her lap. She stroked his hair as he cried himself out, running her fingertips across his scalp as his breathing evened and he fell asleep. It could not have been very comfortable, but she wouldn't have moved him for all the ore in the *Harland*'s hold.

"We'll find a way," Pendt said, as much to herself as anyone else.

Brannick Station hummed around her. Home and safe, very sad, but *hers*. And she would risk everything to keep it that way.

# 21.

**THE FIRST THING PENDT** did was make sure everything was still legal. Not wanting to bother Fisher, she arranged to borrow Dulcie's office for an afternoon. The foreman immediately understood her purpose and granted her access to the files she was going to need. Then Dulcie went to the quartermaster to see about getting Pendt her own workspace—between hydroponics and the apartment, Pendt had never really needed one, but she was forced to admit that Dulcie had a point—and Pendt got to work.

Marriage was such an antiquated concept that she wasn't sure how or if death factored into it. She felt awful, reducing Ned to a line on the page of questions she had to answer, but she had no choice. For the safety of everyone on Brannick Station, she *had* to belong to it.

The documentation was fairly clear cut, all things considered. Dulcie had done countless weddings on the station, but this was her first marriage ever, and she'd made sure to access all the information the historical database would give her, apparently. Pendt had read the contract the day she signed it, but going over it now, she appreciated it thoroughness. She had married Ned, but it was Fisher, as head of the family, who controlled her future. Ned's death didn't change that. She was a Brannick until she died.

Pendt called up the secondary contract, the one Ned had signed to ease his conscience over the whole affair. He'd written it himself, guaranteeing Pendt full rights to her body, her assets, and as much autonomy as the station could allow her. She cried a little bit as she read it. Ned had been so sweet. The two contracts didn't contradict each other, which was what Pendt had been worried about. Her aunt was very good at finding loopholes, and if one existed in the second contract, Pendt had to know in order to prepare herself. But all seemed well enough.

The door hissed, and Dulcie came back into her office.

"Did you find what you were looking for?" she asked.

Pendt ceded her chair to her.

"Yes," she said. "I think we are all safe with the original arrangement."

"That ship of yours," Dulcie said. "There's something not quite right about it."

"You think?" Pendt said.

"I mean, everything is always accounted for perfectly," Dulcie clarified. "In two decades, you'd think there'd be some kind of oversight with the manifest."

"You haven't spent much time with my aunt," Pendt pointed out. "Captain Arkady knows everything about the *Harland*. It's almost uncanny."

"Maybe," Dulcie said. "But what kind of ship that size has an entirely empty hold when it comes into the only large station it encounters in two decades?"

"What?" Pendt said. Then she remembered her passage through the lower hold, how everything was clean and there was no sign of any passengers having spent years living there. "Oh, the lower hold. That's for passengers. They're usually outgoing, to work on the mining colonies."

"If you say so," Dulcie said. "Anyway, the quartermaster has several options for you, whenever you're ready. It's a question of location, really. The places you work on the station are pretty spread out."

"Thank you," Pendt said, accepting the datapad from her. "I'll take a look and think about what I want. It should probably be nearer operations, though. That's where I'm needed the most urgently."

"True enough," Dulcie said.

Pendt bid her goodbye and headed out onto the colonnade. She stopped for a snack at one of the restaurants and sat chewing thoughtfully while she turned her discussion with Dulcie over in her mind. Pendt had been quick to dismiss the foreman's suggestions in conversation, that there was something shady about the *Harland*, but now that she was mulling it over, Pendt was forced to admit Dulcie might be right. She didn't know why she felt so defensive about it. She wasn't a Harland anymore and she was never going back. But she'd been on that ship for almost eighteen years. Whatever took place on board, she was party to, whether she liked it or not.

There was one person who might know. Dr. Morunt resolutely

refused to discuss his sister with her, but maybe if she explained that it was necessary, he would open up. She hated to ask anyone to access painful memories. She knew how difficult they were to bury and unlearn, but she had a feeling she was going to need answers.

Pendt finished her snack and turned in her dishes. Several people came up to her to inquire about her health and Fisher's. She told them that Fisher was doing well—the truth—but that he might be working a bit too hard. This received understanding nods, and she promised everyone that she was keeping an eye on him, which was also true.

Making her way along the colonnade, Pendt took time to look in shop windows and watch station residents go about their business. It was a system she never tired of: the flow of goods made on the station or imported from Katla, the ebb of conversation and movement in the crowd around her. Today it was even more comforting. Ned was gone, but Brannick Station was able to continue to function because of what he had done when he was still alive.

At last, she made her way to the infirmary and ducked into Dr. Morunt's portion of the office. He was sitting at his desk, reading something, and so she coughed politely to get his attention.

"Pendt, a pleasure," he said. "Please, sit."

"I'm not here for a medical reason," Pendt said. "If you have important work to do, I can come back."

"No, it's all right," Morunt said. "I have nothing pressing for a couple of hours, and some conversation would be welcome."

Pendt hoped he still felt that way after she started talking.

"Dr. Morunt, I know this is a difficult time for a lot of us, and

I hate to add pressure to you." Pendt began as diplomatically as she could. "But if you can, if you're able, I need to ask you some questions about your sister."

Morunt stilled in his chair, his face growing several shades paler.

"Foreman Channing has raised concerns about my family's ship," Pendt continued. "And since that would impact my safety and the safety of the station, I was hoping you might be able to help. I know it's not a subject you are comfortable with, and I understand if you kick me out of your office, but please understand: You are the only person who might be able to help me with this. I wouldn't put you in this position if it wasn't important."

Morunt said nothing for a few moments, but he was nodding while he turned her words over in his thoughts.

"All right, Pendt," he said. "I will tell you what I can. I don't know very much."

"Thank you," Pendt said. She leaned back in the chair and considered her words carefully. It was probably best to be direct. "How did your sister come to be on the *Harland*?"

Morunt closed his eyes to the memories. A small smile curled his lips, and Pendt was glad that not all of his recollections were bad ones.

"She was a genius, our Sylvie," he said. "She was the youngest, and my father didn't want her. We were born on Katla, though, so it wasn't much of a strain on him to make sure she was educated. If we'd lived anywhere else, things might have been different."

He paused and took a deep breath.

"Sylvie started following us along to our medical classes when she was about ten," he continued. "Her connection to the æther was about the same as ours, but she had a gift for healing. Eventually the instructors just . . . accepted her into the class. She graduated when she was seventeen."

Pendt tried to imagine the Morunt she knew as a seventeen-year-old prodigy, and it was essentially impossible. Whatever spirit she'd had as a child, the *Harland* had killed off.

"Then the *Harland* came into Katla Station," Morunt said.

"What?" Pendt said. "To Katla?"

"From what my father gathered, it was a very special trip," Morunt said. "They were dropping off something too valuable to trust to another courier. I think that was what drew my father's attention. He always had an eye for opportunities.

"Anyway," he pressed on. "My father spoke to the captain, your grandfather, I believe, and the next thing we knew, Sylvie was dragged out of our quarters and through the *Harland*'s loading bay. Father didn't let her take anything with her, said she wouldn't need it in space. The last I saw my sister, she was screaming against the seal of a Katla airlock. My father had already turned away."

Morunt closed his eyes and two tears ran down his cheeks.

"We couldn't stay with our father after that," he said. "He wanted three sons, and instead he got nothing. After Sylvie left, he could afford a nicer place for us to live, but we all refused. We knew where that money had come from. My two brothers headed towards Hoy, and I came here. It was a foolish hope, but I knew that if I ever saw Sylvie again, it would be at Brannick Station."

"I don't think it's foolish to hope," Pendt said.

"Maybe," Morunt said. "But if my sister ever comes back here, it'll mean she's bringing your family with her, and that's not going to be good for you."

"Your father sold Dr. Morunt to my family." Pendt had to say the words out loud to make it real.

"Yes," he said. "Somehow, he knew that they were buying."

The pieces in Pendt's head began to circle in some semblance of order, the horror of it dawning full.

"It wasn't just your sister they trafficked," Pendt said. "I knew they traded in embryos. It's how all my cousins and siblings and me were born. But it wasn't just that either. We never took passengers on board. Those people who lived in the lower hold weren't going out to Alterra and the other mining complexes by choice. That's why the hold was empty and so clean when we got to Brannick Station: They scrubbed away the evidence of trafficking because someone on Brannick might notice."

"You were a child," Morunt said, quick to absolve her.

"I read messages." Pendt's voice was dull and she curled in on herself. "Over the intercom to the hold below. I told them when and where we'd be arriving. I thought it was to give them hope, but it was to let them know who they'd been sold to."

"It wasn't your fault," Morunt said. His eyes fogged over, and he couldn't meet her gaze. "My father figured it out because he knew what to look for in a smuggling operation, but you couldn't have done that. You couldn't have known."

"It wasn't your sister's fault either," Pendt said. She felt like she was coming apart as her world reordered itself into something even worse than she'd already known. "But she helped them. They would have left her or airlocked her if she hadn't. And I would have helped too, if it meant half a gram more protein on my plate at dinnertime."

Morunt leaned across his desk and took her hands. Pendt felt immediately grounded.

"There is a difference," he said, voice desperate. "Between survival and cruelty."

Pendt wasn't so sure. She had experienced so much of her family's mistreatment in the name of the ship's continued existence. Everything could be counted for on the scales. But the *Harland* wasn't a person. It didn't have feelings. When she was little, Pendt had wanted nothing more than to make the *Harland* happy. It occurred to her for the first time that she never could. It was a *ship*. Her aunt and her mother and her cousins and her siblings—those were the people who had used her, not some ideal of a family legacy that she'd been born to uphold.

"Thank you," she said as her world reordered itself again. She felt freer than she ever had, and it had cost a good person some painful memories. "I—"

"I understand, Pendt." Dr. Morunt held up a hand. "You were trained from birth to take responsibility for things that were never yours to carry. I'm glad I could help you, even if it hurts a bit."

Pendt didn't remember what she said after that or how she made it all the way back to their apartment. When she arrived in the lounge, Fisher was playing a game on the entertainment console, the first time he'd picked it up again since they'd learned about Ned. He set the controller down as soon as he saw her, though, rose, and pulled her into his arms.

"What is it?" he said.

"My family," Pendt said. "The great legacy and secret of the *Harland*. We don't just trade in ore and oglasa. We trafficked human beings. They would have sold me off to the highest bidder for a 'perfect' baby, and then used my body and my æther connection to make more Harlands between contracts."

Fisher's arms tightened around her, holding her steady as the storm of her emotions rocked through her. It wasn't sadness or regret that made her cry. It wasn't even grief. It was pure, incandescent rage, and when she found a way to target it, the *Harland* wouldn't stand a chance.

# 22.

AS PENDT GRAPPLED WITH the realization of what her family's business truly was, Fisher tried to settle his own feelings. It was easier said than done.

He was excruciatingly aware of the fact that Pendt had viewed her relationship with Ned mostly as a business transaction. They had liked each other well enough, which was nice, but both of them had been getting what they wanted. If asked, Fisher would also say he was getting what he wanted. He ran the station now, standing alone for the first time since he was born.

But in the days where he'd got to know Pendt better, before news of his brother's death had arrived, Fisher started to realize that he wanted something else. Pendt was a hard worker and absolutely dedicated to Brannick Station. She understood him without speaking but was just as happy to talk to him. She felt wonderful in his arms, even now when she was upset about something he couldn't start to help her fix. She had this way of cocking her shoulder when she was focused on a plant that flipped his stomach over. He wanted nothing more in the universe than to kiss her again. Possibly, he wanted to kiss her forever.

Except now Ned was dead. And her family was even more monstrous than he'd suspected. She needed his support and his attention, of course, but she was so self-sufficient and so aware of how much space she occupied at any given moment. She seemed reluctant to take any more from him.

But she had kissed him back. That awful day that had started out so well, when he held her on the sofa, and she overbalanced to put all of her weight on his chest. She had kissed him back. Through all of Fisher's grief and concern over the uncertainties of the future, he clung to that feeling.

He missed Ned, would miss him forever. In a way, missing Ned was easier than missing his parents. At least Ned's fate was sure. His parents' lives would always be hanging over him. There was the threat that someday the Hegemony may use his father to open the Net and that would be the end of Brannick Station as he knew it. Missing his parents required Fisher to acknowledge that someday they might come back. Missing Ned required his grief and that was much simpler to give.

Pendt didn't miss the *Harland*. She hadn't before, and she definitely didn't now. But she had to know they'd come back someday. The month was long since up, and now they could literally appear on the scans at any moment. At some point, he supposed, they would have committed to another two-decade run. Maybe that was what Pendt believed. It would certainly keep her sane. She would be nearly forty when the ship came back. The captain might be dead by then.

She and Fisher weren't the same, as Pendt had said, but they could understand each other. Ned always accepted him, but Ned was his brother. Fisher knew that didn't guarantee anything; even before he'd met Pendt, he knew that some families were meaner than his. Pendt's acceptance was different. She had no reason to trust him that day in the bar, but she had chosen to. And she continued to. She said she didn't think she'd ever loved anyone, and maybe she still didn't, but she trusted him, and that wasn't nothing.

Pendt's storm of fury had passed, and when she looked up at him, her eyes were dry. He relaxed his hold on her, giving her the space to put distance between them if she wanted to, but she didn't move away.

"Thank you," she said. "I can't imagine going through this on my own."

"Not to make it transactional," Fisher said lightly, "but I seem to recall at least one time in the past week when you made sure I wasn't going through something hard on my own."

She rubbed her face on his shoulder.

"Anyway," he continued, "I don't mean that I owe you. I'm doing this because I want to. But if it makes it easier for you, you can remember all the things you do for me."

"You know," she said thoughtfully, tracing one finger across his chest, "it doesn't make it easier. I mean, it would have, even just a few weeks ago. But everything has been different since you kissed me. It doesn't feel like give and take. It feels . . . permanent."

Fisher swore his heart stopped beating for a few seconds.

"And you're okay with that?" he asked. He tried not to hold his breath.

"Yes," Pendt said. "It's new for me and it's a bit scary. In a way, it's kind of . . . good? I was worried that you might think I had just transferred my arrangement from Ned to you, but the things I feel now are entirely different from how it was with him."

"I did not think that," Fisher admitted. "But that's possibly because we hadn't had enough time for me to really unpack it yet before, well, you know."

"Will the people on the station think it's weird?" Pendt asked. "Like I'm betraying Ned or, I don't know, taking advantage of you?"

Fisher hadn't considered that either.

"I don't think so," he said after a moment. "They like you for your own sake, now. If anything, I think it would make everyone more comfortable, to know that both of us are making the best of a sad situation and moving forward together."

"Is that what we're calling it?" Pendt asked.

"We don't have to call it anything, if you don't want," Fisher said. "But I would like to sit down again, if you don't mind. I'm exhausted."

She laughed and let him lead her over to the sofa. He sat and pulled her down into his arms again. It was cozy.

"I checked with Dulcie about the legal situation," Pendt said. "Everything is in order. Now that I know what I know about the *Harland*, I realize that legality might not be enough, but it will matter to the station. If the *Harland* can't trade here, they'd be exiled to the mining belt forever."

"I'm tempted to enforce that anyway," Fisher said. "I hate to think that we've been letting people be smuggled through the station, but it's unavoidable. Who knows how many of the ships we've sent out since you got here have been delivering so-called passengers to your aunt? You said your Dr. Morunt is almost sixty. That's too long."

"We can talk to Dulcie about it," Pendt said. "She seemed to be right on the edge of making the same conclusions I did. She didn't know to talk to Dr. Morunt here. We'll have to tell her, and then she can help us."

"I can pass along the information to Ned's rebel contacts too," Fisher said. "The only person I knew was Choria, the captain of the *Cleland*, but if we look through his message history, we might find someone else to talk to. If they aren't already, they can start looking into people being moved from Katla."

"You think the trafficking is that organized?" Pendt said.

"It would have to be," Fisher pointed out. "If the people came from Brannick Station, we would miss them."

That much was true. Brannick had a large population, but it was mostly a series of interconnected families. If there was trafficking going on, someone would have been missed by now.

"I'm still going to poke around," Pendt said. "There has to be someone here who knows what's going on. Someone had to clear out the *Harland*'s lower hold."

"Maybe they were just contracted to clean," Fisher said. "If the hold was already empty, there's no reason for them to know any of the details."

"They might still have seen something," Pendt said. "Even if they didn't know what it was they were doing."

Fisher considered it.

"That's a good point," he said. "I'll go over the schedule and see who was on cleaning duty that day. You can talk to them, or we'll have Dulcie do it if you want to stay a bit anonymous."

Pendt rested her head against his shoulder, and they breathed together. Half an hour ago, everything had seemed to out of control and beyond her, and now they had a plan. Fisher was more than reliable and steady for her, he was the answer to questions she wasn't even sure how to ask.

"Pendt," said Fisher.

"Yes?" she answered, looking up at him again. His eyes were dark.

"I—"Whatever he had planned to say went unheard as Pendt leaned up into him and pressed her lips to his.

This kiss was different from the first one they had shared. Slower, more deliberate, it burned through him. He relaxed into the sofa cushions, taking her full weight against his body. She settled between his legs, her hands on his thighs for balance as she dragged her tongue along his teeth.

She was so tiny, compared with him. He knew it was the result of an underfed childhood, and he tried not to think it was attractive. She'd put on so much weight since she arrived on the station, rounding out her stomach and her hips, and still his hands felt perfectly sized to hold her against his body. She was soft now, her skin having lost its papery feel even as the body underneath it filled out with calories and fat and muscle. This was who Pendt was meant to be, her true form. Not the waif her family had tried to suppress. Not the unwilling mother they would have forced her to be once she turned eighteen. This glorious girl in his lap, her mouth on his with a hunger he could match.

She pulled back, panting for breath, and smiled at him.

"I'm not entirely sure what you want," she said.

"To be honest, neither am I," he told her. "This is new for me as well."

Her smile grew even wider, her hands sliding up his chest to brace herself against his shoulders.

"We'll figure it out," she said. "I have a certain amount of confidence in us."

She said it so matter-of-factly that he blinked. Then he saw the quirk of her lips and realized she was making fun of him. He laughed and pulled her body flush against his. Fisher never wanted to leave Brannick Station, but he had finally found something he wanted to explore.

# 23.

THREE DAYS LATER, FISHER was working in operations when a notification came in. They would need to clear the lower pylons, it said. A generation ship was coming, and that was the only place that it would fit. Fisher held his breath while he read over the specifications. There was no doubt in his mind. It was the *Harland*.

He looked around the room. Dulcie would have gotten the notification, and Pendt as well, but she was spending this shift in hydroponics. It was entirely likely she wouldn't hear the notification chime, if she was busy enough, Fisher thought. He immediately dismissed the lie: Pendt always listened for chimes in case she was needed to open the Well or the Net. The foreman looked up at him, a question written on her face.

"I'll take care of it," he said, and hoped he would be able to.

The *Harland* hadn't been gone long enough to make it anywhere and back, which meant they must have rendezvoused with one of the faster sublight ships Pendt had brought through the

Net. That, or they had been waiting for a message from someone, but from everything he knew of Arkady Harland, she wasn't the type to waste resources, waiting in space. Fisher reread the notes from their departure last time: Yes, someone had mentioned that they were headed to a meeting. No further details were given, but none could really be expected.

The manifest Fisher was given was short. The *Harland* wasn't off-loading anything, but they did have a few scheduled pickups. None of them flagged Fisher's attention when he looked them up in the station's records. He had no idea why they were making this trip.

A supplementary document appeared on the file. It was a notice from First Officer Lodia Harland, stating that the last time the *Harland* had been at Brannick, there was a miscommunication, and one of the ship's hands, her daughter, had been left behind. There was no mention of Pendt by name, just a physical description and a promise that Lodia would reimburse any costs her daughter had incurred while she had stayed on the station. It seemed uncharacteristically generous, to say the least.

No sooner had Fisher finished reading than the door to operations slid open, and Pendt came flying in. Her hair was bound up around her head, tufts sticking out of the scarf she'd wrapped around it to keep sweat and soil from mixing in her hair. There were green smudges on her cheeks and dirt under her fingernails. She'd never looked more alive.

"Did you see this?" she said, brandishing the datapad. Everyone was staring now.

"Yes," Fisher said as calmly as possible. "Do you want to go somewhere and discuss it?"

Pendt seemed to realize there were witnesses. She immediately reined herself in. It would have been painful to watch if it had been her disappearing into a shell, but instead it was as though the professional, adult version of herself stepped forward to deal with the situation.

"Of course," she said. "As long as I am not interrupting?"

The people in operations knew more about Pendt's personal history than the given station worker, and they were almost as protective of her as Fisher was. Furthermore, they took their cues from Dulcie, and the foreman was clearly upset about something. No one would question the interruption.

"We're good," Dulcie said. "I was about to kick Fisher out to get some dinner anyway. He skipped lunch."

"You promised not to tell!" Fisher protested at exactly the same time Pendt said, "You promised you wouldn't do that anymore!"

The operations crew laughed. It was almost normal.

"Come on, then," Fisher said, and led her into the office off the side. It's where Ned had liked working best, because he could be alone there. Fisher preferred to work in the main room.

"There's no way my mother is going to pay you back for everything I've eaten since I got here," Pendt said before the door had sealed. "Let alone the clothes."

"Are you joking?" Fisher asked. "I honestly can't tell if you're joking."

"I'm dead serious," Pendt said. "I don't know what Lodia wants, but I guarantee you that she's not going to pay you for it."

"Pendt," he said, "I meant that isn't my priority. It never even crossed my mind to calculate how much— You know you can't leave anyway, I mean, I couldn't let you leave, even if they offered to pay me what you were worth. Which they can't, because your worth is beyond measure."

It was a bit garbled, but she seemed to get the point.

"Oh," she said. "I panicked and I forgot how things worked."

"Understandable," Fisher said. "What are you going to do when they come here and find out they have no legal hold on you?"

Pendt thought about it.

"Send them on their way, I suppose," she said. "They have no hold on me, and I don't owe them anything because they thought they could come back and claim me. Why, do you think we should try to help them? They might have trouble making the next port on the supplies they've wasted to get back here, but I don't want Brannick Station complicit in their trafficking, now that we know what they're really doing."

"I did wonder if you'd want to help them," Fisher said. "Or if you'd want revenge. Either would be understandable. They're your family and they treated you like shit."

"If we had enough evidence about the trafficking, I'd have the captain charged under station law," Pendt said. "But we don't. All we can do is send them on their way with no help and build the case against them when they're gone."

"We can do that," Fisher said.

Pendt stared out the window of the office into the black void of space.

"You know," she said after a long moment, "I really thought

they might never come back. They told me I was worthless for so long, I guess I thought they would cut their losses with me, even now that I know what I can do."

"They don't know," Fisher said. "And that might be the best revenge."

"Yes," Pendt said. "You might be right."

Any other words of comfort Fisher might have given were stopped by a bright flash outside the window. There should not have been a bright flash outside the window.

"Did something explode?" Pendt said, trying to see.

"No, we would have felt it," Fisher said.

"Then what?" Pendt said.

Fisher's heart sank all the way to his shoes.

"It's the Net."


Operations was calm when they returned to it, but there was an air of panic hanging above everyone's heads.

"Dulcie, it wasn't Pendt," Fisher said calmly. "I don't know how much time we have, but I would like you to evacuate the loading docks and seal every door you can. Have the station populace return to their homes, like a lockdown drill."

To their credit, they still didn't panic. Dulcie announced the drill in a calm voice, while her seconds began to evacuate and seal the docks.

"Pendt—" he started, but she cut him off.

"I am staying here," she told him. "No matter what comes through that Net, I am staying with you."

There was only one person it could be. They knew it, even if no one was willing to say it out loud. This was how the Hegemony invaded. They used their genetic hostage to activate the Net, and then nothing could stop them from arriving at the station of their choice. Fisher's father was coming home, and it was the very worst sort of homecoming imaginable.

The Net glimmered as a ship made contact. Instead of firing its engines and making for a dock on the pylon, it sat there. Eventually, an automatic drone was activated on the station and went to tug the ship in. The whole process was beyond Fisher's control. In the case of station safety, getting a ship to dock was always prioritized, and stopping the drone would require more time to overwrite than they had.

"It doesn't make any sense," said Dulcie. "That's a one-person drone. They can't follow him through."

She was right. The Net was already flickering out, and all of the Brannicks were on this side of it. Nothing could be caught without their say-so.

"Maybe they're using my mother against him," Fisher said.

It was possible, and almost too horrible to contemplate. Pendt knew what her aunt would choose, but Fisher's father actually used his heart.

"I'll go down," Fisher said. "Whatever is going on, I'm the least likely to be hurt."

"I'm coming with you," Pendt said.

"You can't," Fisher said. "You are the station's priority right now. We have to keep you safe."

"Fisher," she said.

"I will be all right," he said. Physically, at least, he was pretty sure. He could already feel his heart starting to fracture. Whatever he found in that pod couldn't possibly be good.

"I'll be watching," she said, indicating the monitors.

"Damn straight," said Dulcie.

Fisher took the lift that let him override all stops between operations and the loading dock where the drone had landed. With the lockdown, it was unlikely that anyone would stop him, but he wanted to be sure. The lift seemed to take forever, even though he knew exactly how long it took. He smiled in what he hoped was a reassuring way for the cameras. Pendt wouldn't be fooled for a moment, but the fact that he was trying would make them all feel a little bit better.

At last, the doors of the lift slid open, and the loading dock spread out before him. The air was already a bit stale, typical when an airlock had cycled during a station lockdown. The drone was ready to open, but whoever was inside wasn't coming out.

Fisher had imagined this moment a hundred—a thousand—times. Good versions, where his parents stepped out smiling and said it was all a misunderstanding. That the Hegemony never meant to split up their family so cruelly. Bad ones, where his father led an army, his mother's blood still staining his hands. Nothing had prepared him for the unknowing of the moment. It was agonizing, and yet he never wanted it to end.

The pod was clearly not going to open itself. Fisher crossed to it and looked at the readings. One life sign, fading. Whoever was inside was injured, but not fatally if they were given medical care. No matter what happened, Fisher told himself, he would help someone today. Even if it came back to bite them.

Since the airlock had already cycled, it was easy enough to open the pod's door. There was no lock on it, no code. It was absolutely ancient, he realized, and he pressed the opening sequence. It was barely space-worthy. Maybe whoever was inside had been healthy when they left and nearly died on the journey.

He was stalling, he knew. He had to get it over with. Pendt would already have it open if she were here. She was probably yelling at him on the viewscreen upstairs.

Fisher finished the sequence and stood back as the door swung open. A rush of oxygen came out, even more stale than the stuff Fisher was breathing, and a body slumped onto the floor of the bay.

Even as he moved forward, Fisher's brain insisted that it wasn't possible. His eyes were deceiving him. The oxygen mix was worse than he'd thought, and he was already hallucinating.

Ned Brannick smiled as his brother pulled him out of oblivion and into his arms. It was such an achingly familiar smile. Fisher wanted to scream. It couldn't be real. It just couldn't. And yet the universe wouldn't be so cruel as to make Fisher lose him twice. Ned collapsed in Fisher's embrace before Fisher could even think of any questions to ask. It was the best thing that had ever happened to him.

"Fisher." Ned's smile faded and he was deadly serious. "Thank goodness. I have some news."

# 24.

BRANNICK STATION WAS STILL locked down, so there were no random bystanders around to watch while Fisher and Pendt hauled Ned to Dr. Morunt's office in the infirmary. Pendt had appeared in the loading bay so quickly Fisher wondered if she'd broken the lift to do it, but he wasn't about to send her away. Together, they could manage Ned, even though he was very unsteady on his feet.

Dr. Morunt was shocked to see the three of them, of course, but immediately helped lift Ned onto the table for an examination.

"I'm fine, I'm fine," Ned protested.

"You are dehydrated," Dr. Morunt said. "And your oxygen saturation is low."

"Put the mask on, Ned," Fisher said. "You can still talk."

Ned put the mask on. His colour was already better with the flow of air normalized, but he was still quite thin. His skin had the papery look to it that Pendt's had when she came aboard. It wasn't because he'd been in space; it was due to malnourishment.

"So the *Cleland* was captured, then?" Pendt asked. Fisher was so grateful that she could keep a level head.

"Yes," Ned said. "We were covering the retreat of several other ships. Choria always volunteers for that sort of thing. It's one of her best qualities."

"We heard it was destroyed with all hands," Fisher said.

"Oh, they destroyed it," Ned said. "But they emptied it first. All our stores went to Hegemony soldiers, and we were taken off to prison. I think they assumed we knew things, but only Choria had any real knowledge of rebel movements, and she never broke."

"And you escaped?" Pendt asked.

Dr. Morunt successfully got an IV line into Ned's arm, and began the flow of nutrients.

"Sort of," Ned said. His face darkened. "We were held in a massive prison in deep space. The only way in or out is by sublight ship. But Choria learned from eavesdropping on the guards that the Hegemony had a wild Well nearby. It takes forever for ships to get there, but once they arrive at the Well, they can aim for any Net they like."

"They still need someone to turn on the Net," Pendt said.

"Well, yes," Ned said. "That's where I came in."

He shifted uncomfortably, trying not to pull at the needle in his arm.

"Choria figured out that I could escape," he said. "You know she's a whiz with calculations. She determined exactly how I'd need to hit the Well to get here, and she knew that the Brannick Station Net would activate for me when I did. It wasn't quite that easy. We had to get a ship for me to go in, but eventually we managed it."

"Well, your timing is impeccable," Pendt said. "We just learned my family is coming back."

Dr. Morunt dropped the equipment he was sterilizing, and an entire tray of medical tools crashed to the floor.

"Doctor?" Fisher asked.

"My apologies," he said. "I'm still a bit in shock."

"That's why I'm here," Ned said. "I heard about the *Harland* while I was at the prison. They've been on the Hegemony's payroll the whole time. Pendt, this might be hard to hear, but they traffic in human beings."

"We know," Pendt said. "We figured it out on our end too."

Ned exhaled so hard the mask shifted on his nose.

"I'm glad you know," he said. "But I'm sorry you had to find out."

"All right, we know they're coming, and we know they're bad news," Fisher said. "I'm glad to have you back, but if that's all the news, then you might have wasted the trip."

He was trying to keep it light, Pendt knew, to fight back the hysteria they were all feeling at seeing Ned, alive, again.

"They know what Pendt can do," Ned said. "They have a Hegemonic order annulling the marriage, and they are going to take her. The Hegemony is going to give them enough money that they'll be able to settle on a *planet* if they want to, and Pendt will belong to the Stavengers."

Fisher felt his legs buckle, and suddenly he was sitting on the floor. Pendt was pale, but kept her feet.

"How?" she said. "How do they know?"

"I told them," said Dr. Morunt. "Your family knows because I told them."

If Fisher could have stood, he might have done murder. Ned bolted upright on the table only to immediately collapse again as Fisher struggled to his knees. By then Pendt was already facing off against the doctor, and it was her fight.

"Why?" she said.

"They told me I could have my sister back," he said. "They let me buy Sylvie, and I answered all of the questions they asked."

"I hope you didn't pay too much," Pendt said, her voice dead as the void. "She's not worth anything to them anymore. You've been fleeced."

Ned was sitting up now, tearing at his IV, but Pendt stopped him. Fisher hauled himself up and turned to the doctor.

"Tell us everything you know," he said.

"They wanted to know how powerful Pendt was," Morunt said. "They asked how she was operating the station, and I told them about the foetus. That's when they got really interested. They asked if you had designed the baby, and I said no, but that you probably could if you had enough calories. That's when they decided to buy you. I said the station would never give you up, that you were *married* of all things, and they couldn't take you. I guess the Hegemony decided to work around its own laws for you."

"I'm flattered," Pendt said. "They want a baby, I suppose? A very specific one?"

"Yes," Morunt said. "I had assumed they wanted a fleet of captains with good star-sense, but Ned's report of a wild Well makes me think the Hegemony is aiming a bit farther."

"They can't," Fisher said as understanding dawned.

"They can," Pendt whispered. "They can give me all the calories

I need and hold me down while they do the implantation. I've seen my aunt do it before—his sister helped. She'd definitely do it again. They'll show me the pattern I'm meant to mimic, and give me a time frame, and then they'll launch me. And either I'll die—"

"Or the Maritech Net will catch you," Fisher finished. "And the Stavengers will have a foothold in that solar system again."

One of the sensors affixed to Ned's chest beeped, and Dr. Morunt moved to take it off him.

"Don't touch me," Ned said, tearing it off himself.

"Dr. Morunt, you have my sympathy," Fisher said. "I don't know what I would have done if the Hegemony had offered me my parents. You will take your sister and you will go to Katla. I don't care where you go after that, but neither of you will be welcome on Brannick Station ever again."

"Thank you," Morunt said. He turned. "Pendt, I—"

She looked at him as cold as the void.

"I understand the difference between survival and cruelty," she said. He bowed his head. "Get out."

Morunt fled, leaving the three of them in the medical bay. Pendt put her hands over her face and took a deep breath. She blew it out hard.

"I need to process this, so try to control yourself even if I say something you don't like," she said to Fisher.

He nodded. Ned did too.

"Worst-case scenario," Pendt said, "they take me. The station is fine, because Ned is here."

"Unacceptable," said Fisher. He caught himself. "Sorry, keep going."

"Brannick becomes the jump point for Maritech, just like the old empire wanted," Pendt continued. "You probably make a good amount of money. Human trafficking definitely increases—"

"Over my dead body," Ned burst out. "I mean, again, I guess. Please, continue."

"You can't hide me," Pendt said. "There's nowhere I can go. My aunt won't care if taking me off the station endangers it. They think Ned's in prison, so they're probably counting on Brannick dying, and then they'll just . . . repopulate it. Probably with soldiers."

"None of this is making me feel better," Fisher said.

"I can't run, I can't hide," Pendt said. "All of the best outcomes require my death."

"What?" This time both boys interrupted her together.

"Brannick still has Ned, so it's fine," Pendt said. "The Stavengers never get a foothold in Maritech, so *that's* fine. My family is bankrupted, and to be honest I don't fucking care. But all of those things only happen when I'm dead."

"We can't just tell them you're dead," Fisher said. "They wouldn't believe a medical certificate or only our word. They'd need a body. The whole station would have to believe it."

Pendt took a long moment to think about it. There was a way. It was risky and it relied on other people choosing to help them. Pendt remembered the slow drip of an IV and years of whispered, clandestine instruction. She remembered the warning, given in enough time for her to save up the calories she would need to get off the ship and disappear into the crowd.

"The captain trusts her Dr. Morunt," Pendt said. "But she was always as good to me as she could be. And we know they'll have her with them. If she's the one to confirm my death, they'll believe her."

"One, that is a *huge* amount of trust to put in someone whose brother just betrayed you," Ned said, "and, two, none of that solves the part where you seem determined to die."

"You didn't stay dead," Pendt pointed out. "We have some time. We might be able to come up with something by the time they get here."

"I think we should keep my return quiet," Ned said. He was uncharacteristically serious. "I'm happy to be the backup chromosome, but I am not going to stay here when all of this is over."

"What are you talking about?" Fisher said. "We just got you back."

"I know," Ned said. "But the people who helped me get out of prison are still back there, suffering. They helped me as a last-gasp attempt to do something good. I can't . . . stay here. I have to go back. I might be more useful to the rebellion dead than I was when I was alive."

Fisher thought his head might explode, and once again, Pendt's cool thinking prevailed.

"We'll solve that problem when we get to it," Pendt said. "Our priority right now has to be faking my death. I wish we could ask Morunt for help, but we can't trust him. We do, however, have complete access to his office until Dulcie lifts the lockdown, so I think we should take advantage of it."

Fisher got on the communications channel with Dulcie, who was beside herself by this point, and relayed a short version of what had been decided: Ned's return was a secret; Pendt's family was bad news. She was instructed to give them another two hours of lockdown before she let the citizens go back to their usual routines.

Pendt scrolled through Morunt's files as Fisher and Dulcie talked, with Ned reading over her shoulder.

"Just get on that terminal and find me anything about hearts or breathing rate or, I don't know, brain atrophy," she said.

"None of those sound like fun," he said, moving to start the task.

"Neither does being impregnated and shoved through a wormhole so that the heirs of a dying empire can fulfill their ancestors' wildest colonial wet dreams," Pendt said. "Frankly, I think death is preferable, but I don't want it. I like living."

"You like Fisher," Ned said. Pendt did not deny it. "That's good. I like that you have each other."

"I'm sorry I'm not, like, normal at being a wife," Pendt said.

"Normal's overrated," Ned said. "And anyway, I'm a rebel, remember? I'm against normal on principle."

"All right, Dulcie's going to buy us some time," Fisher said, coming over to where they were working. "But I want us to be back in the apartment well before the lockdown is over. If someone spots Ned, we're going to have to answer a lot of questions, and I don't think we have time for that."

The three of them scanned datafiles for another hour, adding things to Pendt's datapad they thought might be helpful. Finally, Fisher declared it was time to leave. They made their way back to the apartment, the colonnade ghostly quiet around them. For the first time, Brannick Station felt more like a battlefield than anything else, and Pendt wasn't going to stop until she had won back her home.

# 25.

AFTER THREE DAYS OF reading, Pendt decided she knew more about the human body than she'd ever wanted to.

"This is why I work with plants," she groused as Ned brought her orange juice and toast. The boys were knocking back cups of stimulant, but Pendt didn't drink anything stronger than mint tea.

"I am kind of grossed out," Ned said. "Like, I knew that people died, but I didn't know there were so many options."

"There aren't, really," Fisher said. "Most traumas result in death by heart attack."

"I hate you," Ned said, and pressed his face into a pillow.

"Maybe we're coming at this backwards," Pendt said. "We're focusing on ways to die, but maybe we should be looking at ways to resuscitate me."

"I don't want to actually kill you," Fisher said. "I thought we were just going to get you really, really close."

"We haven't found a way to do that yet," Pendt said. "So maybe it would be easier to just get it over with and focus on bringing me back."

"Well, it's not like you've died before and can tell us," Ned said. "I've only died for paperwork. Fisher's never even come close."

"I did come close," Pendt said. "When I was little and regrew my fingernail? I almost died. I had spent too many calories, and they had to bring me back. There was time enough for them to debate if they should, and then Dr. Morunt was allowed to start the IV line."

"How does that help us?" Fisher asked.

"Have you ever used more calories than you have to tap the æther?" Pendt asked. Both boys shook their heads. "Start looking for that in the research. Any kind of mage, but search for people who used up too much magic and fell into a coma as a result."

Neither of them protested. The new search parameters brought up a bunch of stuff they'd already read, so it took them a while to sift through it again.

"I might have something," said Pendt after a couple of hours. "This is a theory of what happened when the old Stavenger Empire made the gene-locks. The æther was dying or dead at the time, so they needed every mage they could get their hands on. Most of them died, but some apparently survived."

She sent the article to their datapads, and they read it as quickly as they could.

"Pendt, this is fringe science at best," Fisher said. "There are only four sources, and three of them are by the same author."

"It's the best thing we have," Pendt countered.

"Please explain it to me like I've recently almost died of void exposure," Ned requested. Pendt smiled at him. He was working as hard as the rest of them, and he was still exhausted.

"The mages who didn't die went into comas," Pendt said. "And most of them never woke up. But the ones who were tended to medically did. If treatment was started immediately, their chances increased."

"There's no point in faking your death if we have to treat you immediately," Fisher argued. "They'll notice."

"Let me think," Pendt said. She stared at Ned. "There was no body at Ned's funeral, but if there had been, what would we have done with it?"

"I would have been embalmed," Ned said. "And then they would have laid me out in the colonnade for a week or so, so that anyone who wanted to pay respects, could. Embalming is a sign of respect. If they froze me, for example, I could be recycled. But about all you can do with an embalmed body is bounce it off the Well when the funeral's done and send it into space forever."

"That's a little bit gruesome," Pendt said.

"What does your family do?" Ned countered.

"You don't want to know," Pendt told him.

"None of this solves the problem of you being DEAD!" Fisher roared suddenly. "Why am I the only person who is bothered by that?"

"We're all bothered, Fisher," Pendt said. "I show it by getting very calculating and your brother shows it with inappropriate humour."

Fisher laughed darkly.

"All right," Pendt said. "I expend a lot of calories on the æther.

You hook me up to embalming fluid immediately. We can alter the formula so that it's more of a restorative than a preservative but keep it very low grade. My family comes to view my body, and you tell them that the embalming is for station tradition. Dr. Morunt confirms my death. The *Harland* leaves. You bring me back. Ned and I are both legally dead and start over."

"I hate it," Fisher said.

"I know," Pendt said.

"What about the foetus?" Ned asked.

"I'm not sure," Pendt said. "There's a lot of risk in this plan, for both of us."

"You are our priority, with Ned here," Fisher said. Ned agreed. "We will focus on saving you."

"All right," Pendt said. "What do you think I should use the æther for?"

"What?" Fisher said.

"Well, if I'm going to do a lot of magic, it might as well be on something useful," Pendt said. "I'm not just going to turn all the grain in hydroponics purple. It'll have to be something huge."

The three of them sat in the lounge, raking through their dreams for anything they could think of that might be big enough.

"You could change Fisher." Ned sounded hesitant, like he was voicing something he knew wasn't quite right, but that someone had to say. "You could give him the chromosome he needs to run the station by himself."

Fisher didn't say anything.

"You know it's never made a difference to me, in terms of who you are," Ned said. "But . . . would it make you happy?"

"I don't know," Fisher said.

"He *is* happy," Pendt said. She blinked several times, and her eyes flashed. "He is already happy. He knows who he is, and he has made a place for himself. It's not fair to ask him to change."

"We asked you to change," Fisher said. "You said yourself, you didn't want to be a mother yet, and yet you made yourself one for us."

"For the station," Pendt said. "The station needed me."

"And it doesn't need Fisher?" Ned said.

"It *has* Fisher," Pendt said.

"Why is this upsetting you so much?" Fisher asked. "You're allowed to take risks and make sacrifices, but I'm not?"

"Because you shouldn't have to change!" Pendt said. "You're perfect the way you are. The universe has pushed me around my entire life, always playing the card that makes me trust its cold calculus and choose against my feelings, but I won't. Not this far. I will not change the person I love because some long-dead despot thought that one chromosome was easier to control than another."

If words could have lit the æther on fire, she'd have been burning.

"You . . . love me?" said Fisher.

"I—" Pendt's voice failed her.

"You two are adorable." Ned clapped his hands. "I'm so glad I died and brought you together."

"Shut up," said Fisher.

"The fact remains," Pendt said, "I won't change you, or anyone else for that matter, to make you into a key to fit a lock that was forced upon us. I'd rather change—"

Her eyes widened.

"Fisher," she said, the galaxy open to her every bidding. "Where is the gene-lock?"

It took them several hours to find it. At first, they pored over blueprints of the station until they realized that the entire point of hiding something was to take it off the plans. They tried looking for gaps, then spaces, where something magical might fit.

"It has to be a physical thing," Pendt said. "Or it would have stopped working when the rest of the Stavenger magic did. Like the Net and Well, it's an actual object and they put æther on top of it. If we find it, we might be able to manipulate it the same way."

"I don't think Brannick genes are going to get you into the Brannick gene-lock," Ned said. "That wouldn't be very secure."

"No," Pendt said. "But I don't need a key. I'm going to change the lock itself."

Eventually Fisher had to reach out with his own æther connection, the electricity magic he rarely had call to use. With the blueprints as a guide, he followed the ebb and flow of power on the station until he found a place with a lot of power for no reason.

"That must be it," Ned said. It was a small cabinet in one of the mechanical bays. Power fluctuations were fairly regular there, as things were charged or shorted out during the repair process. That's why no one had ever noticed. Pendt could walk right up to the lock and lay her hands on it, if she wanted.

"What will happen when you break it?" Fisher asked.

"I'm not going to break it," Pendt said. "Mostly because we

don't know what will happen. I can't exactly experiment with a station full of people. But I can *change* it. I can tie it to the Brannick DNA without using the Y chromosome for control. It sounds small, but it's going to be the biggest thing I've ever tried to do."

"I believe you," said Fisher. "And after?"

"After, you and Ned will both be able to work the Net and Well," Pendt said. "And so will I, if the foetus and I both survive the effort."

"We're going to do everything we can," Ned said.

"I appreciate that," Pendt said. "I'm going to start calculating how many calories I'll need to consume, both before and after. I should be able to figure out the numbers, but there's a slight amount of chance involved here. It might not work, or there might be complications."

"You could have a heart attack," Fisher said.

"Amongst other things," Pendt agreed. "But I still think it's our best shot."

"The timing is going to be really specific," Ned said. "We'll have to have the *Harland*'s arrival down to the minute."

"I can factor it into my math," Pendt told him.

"I thought this was something you just knew," Fisher said.

"It is," Pendt said. "But I want to be sure. And also, I want to leave directions for you two. If it were me watching, I'd feel better if I understood the whole process. Would you rather not?"

"No," Ned said. "I want to know every step."

"Me too," Fisher said.

"It's a best-case scenario plan," Pendt said. "If Dr. Morunt tells Arkady I'm revivable, I don't have a contingency."

"We trust you," Ned said before Fisher could say anything to further complicate the matter. "We'll have to trust her as well."

Pendt began to calculate the number of calories she expected to spend to get enough æther through her system to change the lock. The amount was staggering. It made her stomach queasy thinking about having to ingest so much, even though much of it would be intravenous. She separated the number into before and after, the calories she would need to prepare and the calories she would require to pull herself back. She tinkered with the formula for the embalming fluid until she found something a scanner would think was for the dead but would actually help the living. It was barely enough to sustain her, but it would let her hold on for long enough.

She read the numbers back to the boys. They didn't really understand them, so she rephrased them as actual food types to give them something to picture. Ned put his hand on his stomach in sympathy. Eating was fun, but this was going to suck.

Fisher took her hands in his when she was done and squeezed them, as though to reassure himself that she was real, and she was here. She leaned forward to press her forehead against his. She could hear all the things he wanted to say, and she appreciated him so much for not saying them. She wanted to be free of the *Harland* forever, and that was going to take an incredible risk. She loved Fisher—she knew it now—and she loved him in part because he trusted her enough to let her do this.

Ned gave them space, even though he too was clearly on edge

about the whole thing. He checked his communications. The only person who could send him anything right now was Dulcie. There was a notification from her.

"Operations says the *Harland* is due in four days," Ned reported, looking up from his datapad. "Is that enough time?"

"It'll have to be," Pendt said. "I'll make a schedule."

"All right then," Ned said. "What do you want for dinner?"

# 26.

PENDT STARTED TO REGRET her decision on the third solid day of eating. She had to be careful about it: too much and she'd vomit, too little and her body would turn it into regular waste. She could feel every calorie in and out, measured every effort she took against the efforts she was going to make with the energy she had when the *Harland* arrived, and she hated it. It was, she realized, the life she was destined for if this didn't work. If the Hegemony got her, she doubted they'd be as nice about it as Fisher and Ned were.

The *Harland* drifted ever closer on the charts. Pendt had begun exploration of the gene-lock, carefully exploring it without triggering anything that might shut it down. She was paranoid enough to assume the Stavengers had left traps around it, but no matter which angle she took, she couldn't see any.

"It was the last thing they did," Ned reminded her. "They couldn't exactly come out here and check it. They just made it work."

It was a valid point.

Still, she was very careful as she circled closer and closer to the centre of the gene-lock's pattern. She knew what Ned's chromosome looked like, of course. She carried a copy of it inside her. It was a matter of picking the lock far enough to *find* the chromosome, and then changing the specific tumbler without disturbing anything else.

"Does it help to picture it like that?" Fisher said. "It just confuses me."

"Yes," Pendt said. "It's how I think about the Net and Well, so it makes sense to me to think of it like this. I know the pattern and I know the key. Usually I just turn it, but the principle is the same. It helps me reason out how I'm going to do it."

The airlocks would take two hours to cycle after the *Harland* docked. Pendt was sure that would be enough time, and Dulcie said they could always manufacture a stall if they had to, without raising too much suspicion. The foreman was the only other person on board who knew what they were trying, and while she wasn't exactly thrilled about it, she wouldn't stop them either. Dr. Morunt was under unofficial house arrest in his quarters and would not be permitted out until it was time for him to meet with his sister. Pendt did not believe he would betray them any further, but Fisher pointed out that if they used the other Morunt as leverage, he could become unpredictable. Fisher needed to control as much of this as he could, Pendt knew, and so she stopped arguing.

The *Harland* came in exactly on schedule, so Pendt was already sitting in the repair bay with Ned when it docked. Fisher had to be in operations to make everything look normal, which she knew was driving him up the wall. He'd come down as soon as he could.

"Airlock cycle starting now," said Dulcie over their private communications. "Good luck."

"Pendt?" That was Fisher. "Are you still there?"

"I'm just about to start," she told him, "but I knew you'd want to talk first."

"Just . . . be careful, okay?" he said. "And, Ned, do whatever you can."

"I will," Pendt said. "Charge Arkady twice the normal docking fee for me."

"I love you too," Fisher said, and the channel clicked off.

"Well?" said Ned. Pendt held her hands up to the plate behind which was the gene-lock that ruled their lives. "Dying's not all it's cracked up to be. I don't recommend it."

"I'll keep that in mind," Pendt said. She started to reach for the familiar pattern, so close to her heart. "See you on the other side."

*She stretched.*

*She twisted.*

*She found her way through.*

*It was as simple as she thought. X marks the spot.*

*But it was hard. So hard to actually do.*

*She hadn't eaten enough.*

*There wasn't enough food in the whole galaxy.*

*A body couldn't hold it.*

*A soul could.*

*Isn't that what she had learned?*

*That there was something about human life that changed the
    rules?*

*Something that made people choose to do the right thing when it*
   *was hard.*
*The hard thing when it hurt.*
*The hurtful thing because they liked the pain.*
*Messy and complicated.*
*Full of life.*
*Full of love.*
*Full of something, at last, for once in her whole life.*
*She found the thread she needed.*
*And pulled.*

Captain Arkady Harland walked off her ship like she had con-
quered Brannick Station. The boy who was left here couldn't cause
her any trouble, even with her idiot niece trying to pull his strings.
He was alone, and she was powerful. Everything in the universe
turned towards her right now. It was her time.

Beside her, Lodia was almost as determined. If she'd ever felt
anything for the girl she bore, space had driven it out of her. It had
been years since Arkady had been bothered by flashes of maternal
instinct. She felt none when Tanith's baby was born with no connection to the æther and she'd ordered it spaced. Lodia had borne
children more recently than her sister, but she was still a Harland.
She knew how to act.

The Brannick boy stood alone, waiting for them. He looked almost bored. Whatever Pendt had conned him into doing, he clearly
had no idea what he was getting involved with. Probably she didn't
either. Arkady had spent a lot of time keeping her in the dark.

"Captain Arkady, welcome back," Fisher Brannick said. "We

weren't expecting you for some time, of course, but we're always happy to see familiar ships in port."

It was a canned greeting, stale as recycled air.

"We received your supplementary message," he continued. "I'm afraid your request to take your niece back with you cannot be fulfilled."

Arkady grinned. No idea at all.

"I have a document here signed and witnessed by the Stavenger Hegemony," she said, brandishing her datapad in his face. "It annuls the ridiculous marriage between our two families and returns custody of Pendt to me. So much the better, I'm sure you'll agree. She clearly cannot be trusted to make her own decisions."

A muscle in the boy's cheek twitched. The fool had come to *like* Pendt Harland.

"It doesn't matter what documents you have," Fisher said. "Your niece is dead. We think she panicked when she heard your ship had docked, and she tried to connect to the æther and overextended herself. She's on a slab in medical right now, if you want to see her."

"Dead?" said Lodia. "But she— We need her to— She can't—"

"Take us to your medical facility immediately," Arkady ordered. "Lodia, remain here and make sure the other exchange does not take place until I return. Fetch Dr. Morunt. I want her with me."

Pendt's mother nodded and went back to the ship.

Arkady was furious by the time they arrived in medical. It made Fisher feel a bit better. At least she was distracted and not coming up with ways to humiliate him. She hadn't asked how the station was still operating, but maybe his Dr. Morunt hadn't given up all their secrets after all. The *Harland*'s Dr. Morunt was quiet. She had to know that if Pendt was dead, Arkady was unlikely to let her go. It was so much trust to place in a woman he didn't know, but Pendt seemed sure of her.

"This way, please." Fisher ushered them into the bay where Pendt had been laid out. Dulcie was with her, monitoring the feeds and changing the "embalming" fluid as necessary. Ned was somewhere close by, Fisher was sure. "Here she is."

"What are you doing to her?" Dr. Morunt asked.

"She was married to the Brannick," Fisher said. "Our people expect a public funeral. This is how we prepare her for it."

"Check," Arkady gritted out.

Dr. Morunt stepped forward and put her hands on Pendt's chest. She was so, so still. Fisher could barely look at her. The IV dripped, and he hoped, but it was still very hard to watch.

Morunt pulled back from the body.

"She's dead, Captain," Morunt confirmed. "The embalming process has already started to work."

She looked right at Fisher when she said it and blinked very slowly. Arkady was too incensed to notice. Fisher knew it wasn't a power play on the doctor's part. It was a choice to be better. He wished he could give her the world, and was even more grateful to her, because she had to know he couldn't.

"Take us back to the *Harland*," Arkady snapped at Fisher. She grabbed the doctor by the arm, squeezing hard. "I'll tell your brother the deal is off."

Sylvie Morunt didn't say another word, all the way back to the docking bay. It was the longest wait of Fisher's life, watching them cycle through the airlock. He went back to operations and walked them through their departure like it was a normal one. He didn't ask where they were going. He didn't think Arkady knew.

The moment the *Harland*'s engines flared to life, pushing it away from the station at speeds too fast for it to return anytime soon, Fisher was off like a shot. He was out of his chair and running for the lift. No one got in his way. The trip back to medical took just as long as everything else seemed to take on this day of extended eternities, but finally he was there.

Pendt still lay on the medical cot, but Dulcie had switched her IV for something more healthy than the fluid they'd used to fool Arkady. Ned was hovering beside her, holding her hand as the drip of nutrients restored their hope to her blood. He looked up when Fisher came in.

"Gone?" he asked.

"Gone," Fisher said.

Ned put his head on Pendt's chest and breathed deeply, like he was trying to put the world back in order.

"We've almost done it," Ned said. "Now it's up to her."

"It's always been up to her," Fisher said, and it was true.

This girl who came to him from the middle of space and learned how to love for his sake. She was the most wonderful person he had ever met. He needed her. He needed her to wake up. Fisher stepped up to the side of the cot opposite his brother and took Pendt's shoulder. Her hand was full of needles, and he didn't want to disturb any of them.

"Pendt, my amazing girl, they're gone. They're gone for good," he said. "It's safe now, and I need you to wake up. Please. Please wake up."

*It was hard.*
*It was the hardest thing she'd ever done.*
*The job was finished.*
*She had been successful.*
*The lock was changed.*
*The boys were safe.*
*The station was safe.*
*She could rest.*
*NO.*
*NO.*
*NO.*
*She couldn't rest yet.*
*She had more things to do.*
*Pendt Brannick, who had been a Harland and had learned which*
    *parts of that she wanted to carry, began to pull herself out of*
    *the abyss.*

"Wake up, Pendt," Fisher said. "We have a station to run."
Green eyes opened.

# 27.

THE DAY NED BRANNICK left the station of his birth the second time was unremarkable. He was dead, after all, and very few people had known about his return. The most complicated part was finding a new group of rebels that would take him in, but his supposition had been correct: As a dead man who had escaped from one of the Hegemony's most mysterious prisons, he was quite useful to the cause. His new captain made him no promises about when or if an attempt would be made to rescue the surviving crew of the *Cleland*, but Ned didn't expect one. This time, he had a better idea of what he was getting into.

Only Pendt had come down to see him off. Fisher was up in operations, where he was needed to work the Well.

"Try to send us the occasional message this time," Pendt said, throwing her arms around his neck.

"Can two dead people write to each other?" Ned asked, grinning. It was his favourite joke.

"They'd better," Pendt said. "Or your brother will kill us both again."

Ned had no last name now. He hadn't picked one yet. He didn't need one for the register on this ship, and Brannick was too obvious. Pendt Harland was no more, either. Pendt Brannick had taken her place.

"Maybe you can come and visit," Ned said. "Separately, of course."

Brannick Station was slightly more secure now, with two inhabitants able to control the gene-lock. Pendt and Fisher would never be able to leave the station together, but neither would they both be trapped here forever.

"We might," Pendt said. She had other plans, but she didn't doubt their paths would cross again someday.

Ned picked up his few belongings and his new weapons chest and walked up the ramp to the airlock. The captain had not come out to meet him, but a crew member stood waiting for him.

"Goodbye, Ned," Pendt said. It was a simple farewell for anyone who was watching. The previous night, when the brothers had spoken, was much more emotional.

"Goodbye, Pendt," he said.

She waited until the airlock was finished cycling, and then she took the lift up to operations, where Fisher was beginning to coordinate the departure. She watched him work, so happy for him that she thought she might burst.

"Calculations are cleared, Fisher," said one of the techs. "Whenever you're ready."

Fisher smiled and turned the key. The lock recognized him,

and the Well flared to life. The rebel ship streaked towards its destination, leaving rainbows of light in its wake. As the ship disappeared, Fisher breathed out.

"I don't think I'll ever get tired of that," he said. Pendt crossed the floor and took his hand.

"I'm sure the people who live here will be glad to hear it," Pendt said.

The operations staff laughed. Pendt squeezed his fingers and pulled him towards the office so they could speak in private.

"I can't believe Ned is gone again," Fisher said once the door closed. Pendt began to make them tea. "I mean, of course I can. It's just, I was used to him being alive and here, and now he's gone. I have so many questions for him about the station. Things I didn't even know to ask before you changed everything."

"You'll figure it out," Pendt said. "We'll figure it out. We'll make a new system and iron out the bugs as we find them."

"Dulcie will kill us if we mess with the schedule again," Fisher said.

"I think I've worked it all out," Pendt said, a bit defensively. "And anyway, she told me she likes the changes, now that people are starting to settle into them."

She brought the tea over. Fisher took both cups out of her hands and set them on the side table so he could pull her into his lap. She didn't resist.

"I miss him too," she said, resting her head against his shoulder. "And I worry about him, even though he's only just left. And in a way, that makes me happy. I had five brothers, and not a single one of them cared about me. Now I have one, and he's perfect."

"I'm really glad he didn't hear you say that," Fisher said. "He's already insufferable."

Pendt laughed. Fisher took a sip of tea. It wasn't so bad.

"I want to break the lock on the station," Pendt said. Fisher was glad he was already sitting down. "I know we can't do it here. There are too many unknowns. But if I can find a way to get to Enragon Station, then I can experiment a bit more."

"That would take years," Fisher said. "I feel like we just got to settle down a bit."

"It wouldn't take years if I had the Enragon heir with me," Pendt said. "There's been rumours of their heirs forever, and Katla is as good a place to start looking for them as any. People go in and out of there more frequently than they do here, and it'll be easier to escape people's notice if I'm some random researcher on a highly populated station."

"I feel like everyone goes to Katla," Fisher said.

In a way, he was right. They'd deported Dr. Morunt as soon as the dust settled. Pendt had done it, so as not to sully the memory of Fisher's first time using the Well. Katla was the first stop for Ned too. Pendt wouldn't see either of them in all likelihood. Katla Station was much bigger than Brannick.

"Well, I'm not going right away," she said. "I have some things I want to do here first."

"Oh, really?" Fisher said. He slid his hands around her waist.

"Not that," Pendt said, and then amended her answer: "Not *only* that."

Fisher laughed and kissed her. Pendt wrinkled her nose but didn't stop him.

"We've got time," she said. "We'll finish changing our world, make sure everything is in working order. Then we'll see what we can do for everyone else."

Pendt Brannick was eighteen years old, and she could touch the very stars.

# EPILOGUE

**ON KATLA STATION, THERE** was a laboratory crammed full of strange equipment and reams of technical readouts that few people could fully understand. There were odd sounds and lights that stayed on deep into the nightshift, whether or not anyone was present. Several dead plants did their best to bring some sense of green life to the room. In the middle of the organized chaos, there sat a girl. Her name was Morgan Enni. And she had things to do.

# ACKNOWLEDGMENTS

This one was rough.

Thank you to Josh Adams, who never gave up on this book, and to Andrew Karre, who never gave up on ME, even when everything was falling apart. Thank you also to the team at Penguin, especially Melissa Faulner, who made miracles happen on short notice over and over again. Anne, you're the best. Anna Booth, thank you for beautiful book design and for double-checking my genetics. Jeff Langevin and Maria Fazio, I don't know how you saw the inside of my brain before I was finished designing it, but you did, and I love the colours.

Thank you to Emma, who put up with an *incredible* amount of waffling on this book, and to Emmy, Rachel, Katherine, Kat, Tessa, and Vee, who read early ("early") versions and reminded me to land all the shots that I had set up. Team #brokenhome and #stealtheunicorn 5eva.

Thank you to the city of Stratford, Ontario, for keeping it together during Covid so that I could sort of keep it together during Covid and manage to write a book. Special shout-out to the

Red Rabbit, Pollo Morta, Mone-Thai, and Barr's Chocolate. You all know why. If you are one of the teens who worked at the Zehrs and meet me in the street, tell me and I will buy you dinner. Or write you a recommendation letter. Or something.

Thank you to Kristen Ciccarelli (and Joe and Yonder). You welcomed me into your home and let me stare at the ocean through your window and pester your neighbours about cod. I love all three of you (even the one who makes me sneeze!).

Is it weird to thank Dragon Age? It has fixed me twice, so I probably should. God, I love those games. I'm glad they reassembled the storytelling parts of my brain (and that I can spinny-stab).

Addy-girl, I love you so much. You were my brightest star in 2020, and I cannot *wait* to watch you take over day care. (Griffey, if it were up to me, you would ALWAYS have Popsicles, but unfortunately that kind of decision-making is above my pay grade, I'm sorry.)

*Aetherbound* was born on an Air Canada cocktail napkin at O'Hare Airport in 2015, carried around in the author's jean jacket pocket for several years, rebirthed on the Trans-Canada Highway somewhere in the middle of New Brunswick, and written with no small amount of agony during phase 3 of pandemic lockdown.

I love you all, and I hope you have enough to eat.